The man holdi[ng] noise.

The next instant h[e] clutching his face.

Beth held a canister of pepper spray in her outstretched hand. Corbin dived into his car and roared out of the space, positioning the passenger side before Beth. He leaned over the console and pushed open the door. "Get in!"

She scooped up her purse, her frightened gaze swinging between him and her car.

The pepper-sprayed man had reached the getaway vehicle. Still blinded, he fumbled with the handle.

Beth shook her head. "No."

"Get in!" Corbin ordered. "There's no time."

A bullet ricocheted off the hood.

The getaway driver had a gun. The noise propelled her forward. She leaped into the passenger seat as another bullet shattered the windshield of her car. Beth threw her arms over her face and crouched behind the dash.

Corbin sped down the garage ramp in Reverse. When they reached the next level, he spun the wheel. The tires squealed and smoked, circling the car forward.

"Put on your seat belt," he ordered gruffly. Glancing at the review mirror, he caught sight of the car following them. "Hang on. This might get bumpy."

Sherri Shackelford is an award-winning author of inspirational books featuring ordinary people discovering extraordinary love. A reformed pessimist, Sherri has a passion for storytelling. Her books are fast paced and heartfelt with a generous dose of humor. She loves to hear from readers at sherri@sherrishackelford.com. Visit her website at sherrishackelford.com.

Books by Sherri Shackelford

Love Inspired Suspense

No Safe Place

Love Inspired Historical

Return to Cowboy Creek

His Substitute Mail-Order Bride

Montana Courtships

Mail-Order Christmas Baby

Prairie Courtships

The Engagement Bargain
The Rancher's Christmas Proposal
A Family for the Holidays
A Temporary Family

Cowboy Creek

Special Delivery Baby
Cowboy Creek Christmas
"Mistletoe Bride"

Visit the Author Profile page at Harlequin.com for more titles.

No Safe Place

SHERRI SHACKELFORD

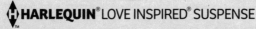

⟨H⟩ **HARLEQUIN**® LOVE INSPIRED® SUSPENSE

Recycling programs for this product may not exist in your area.

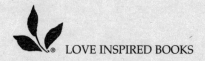

LOVE INSPIRED BOOKS

ISBN-13: 978-1-335-67874-4

No Safe Place

This edition published by arrangement with Love Inspired Books.

® and TM are trademarks of Love Inspired Books, used under license. Trademarks indicated with ® are registered in the United States Patent and Trademark Office, the Canadian Intellectual Property Office and in other countries.

www.Harlequin.com

Printed in U.S.A.

For what shall it profit a man, if he shall gain
the whole world, and lose his own soul?
—*Mark* 8:36

To Jessica Alvarez and TR, my partners in crime!

ONE

Today was a good day to die, as far as days went.

Beth Greenwood focused on the steady *blink-blink-blink* of the cursor on her screen. One click and her life changed forever, possibly even guaranteeing her death unless she disappeared indefinitely. As her trembling index finger hovered over the mouse button, she glanced at the single photo perched on the bare expanse of her desk. Her dad's unwavering stare gave her courage.

Her heartbeat stuttered, and her palms grew damp.

A Chicago cop, he'd suffered a debilitating stroke two months before his retirement. His death had been shattering, but knowing he was no longer suffering gave her a modicum of peace. Never much for talk, Officer Greenwood had lived his faith and had led by his example. Though his job had exposed him to temptation, he'd seen his dedication to truth as a higher moral calling. *For what shall it profit a man*, he'd quote the Bible, *if he shall gain the whole world, and lose his own soul?*

What, indeed? She checked the email attachment and then clicked the option to schedule the message for arrival the morning after the bank holiday. A muffled thump startled her upright, and her pulse thrummed in her ears.

She whipped around, shooting her mouse off the side of the desk, searching for signs of a lingering coworker. The building usually emptied early on the Friday afternoon before a holiday. She leaned out of her cubicle, and her shoulders sagged. An overflowing trash bin sat in the center of the aisle. Probably the cleaning crew getting an early start on the weekend. She retrieved her battered mouse and set it beside her keyboard.

She logged out of her computer with a few rapid clicks, then stood and reached for her dad's photo. She'd supplied the FBI with the evidence she'd discovered about the money laundering. It was time to disappear from Quetech Industries for good.

Not that she'd miss the place.

Her job as a forensic accountant was transient by nature, and she'd worked in plenty of office buildings over the years. Quetech Industries had earned the dubious title of being the worst. It was like drowning in a sea of gray. The walls were medium gray. The carpet was dark gray. Even the cubicles were fashioned from light gray plastic.

She turned and ran into a solid male chest.

Stifling a shriek, she stumbled backward. "Clark, I mean, um, Corbin. What are you doing here this late on a Friday?"

She smoothed her hair with quaking fingers.

"I could ask you the same, Beth," he said, his voice low and intimate, like the romantic strains of a cello.

The ladies in the building had dubbed the new financial consultant "Clark Kent." The office nickname suited his darkly handsome good looks. His coffee-colored hair was cut in neat, almost military, precision, and his eyes were ice-blue behind his black-rimmed glasses. Though he wore a suit and tie, someone claimed they'd seen a sleeve tattoo on his left arm. There was even talk that he was ex-military. Special Forces.

"I was just leaving." Hiding her unsteady hand, Beth reached for her bag. "Had to finish up some work before the weekend."

Corbin had loosened his tie and unbuttoned his collar. He rested his elbow on the top of the cubicle wall, and she caught a hint of ink at his wrist. Her mouth went dry. In another time and place, she'd have been curious about the rest of the art. She had no trouble believing he'd once been in the military.

"You up for a drink?" he asked. "The finance department is meeting at O'Malley's tonight."

"I don't drink," she said, casting a surreptitious glance at the blank computer screen.

She certainly didn't have time to socialize. Someone was laundering money through Quetech Industries to an offshore account. As a forensic accountant, she'd sent white-collar criminals to federal prison in the past. People who laundered money didn't frighten her. Greed and cowardice mostly went hand in hand.

The name of the offshore bank listed on the company's balance sheet, Cayman Holdings Limited, had struck pure terror into her heart.

She could have walked away. She probably should have walked away. She couldn't. The words of Mark 8:36 prevented her: *For what shall it profit a man, if he shall gain the whole world, and lose his own soul?*

"I don't drink, either," Corbin said. "Janice, Matt Shazier's assistant, promised to sing karaoke. We can be the sober witnesses."

Matt was the company CEO, and she couldn't imagine his buttoned-up assistant belting out a tune on a Friday night.

"Sorry." Trying to appear casual, Beth slid this afternoon's department store purchase into her bag. Escaping the building for a little shopping this afternoon had been a welcome respite from constantly looking over her shoulder. "I have other plans."

Two years before, she'd noticed some odd transactions concerning Cayman Holdings on an account she was auditing for another company. Her mentor, Timothy Swan, had offered to review the files. After studying the case, he'd warned her against pursuing the matter further. He'd contacted the FBI, but Beth sensed he was frightened. They'd found his dead body a month later.

The coroner had ruled the forensic accountant's death a murder by poisoning. Not even the FBI had been able to protect Timothy. Which meant the sooner she disappeared, the better. Except Corbin's tall frame and broad shoulders were currently blocking her exit.

"Maybe we can meet tomorrow?" Corbin shrugged. "There's a new coffee house on Fifth Street."

His words gradually penetrated the fog of her anxiety. She was a temporary contractor. Coworkers didn't ask her out for drinks.

She narrowed her gaze. Corbin was a new hire, and he'd been awfully curious about her work. Had he been sent to spy on her?

"Like a date?" she asked.

"Whatever you want to call it."

Adrenaline coursed through her veins. This was bad. This was very bad. Men like Corbin did not ask forensic accountants on dates unless they wanted something. She'd learned that lesson the hard way.

Beth neatly sidestepped around him. "I'm b-busy tomorrow."

And for the foreseeable future. The message she'd sent was time-stamped for delivery on the Tuesday morning following Columbus Day. She had the three-day weekend to disappear before the FBI received the evidence. Three long days before the men who poisoned Timothy discovered they'd been exposed and started looking for her.

She had no illusions about keeping her part in the whistle-blowing quiet. There was no way of turning over the evidence without tipping her hand.

Corbin's brow furrowed above the bridge of his glasses. "Is something wrong?"

"Just anxious to start the weekend."

She spun on her heel and promptly struck the trash bin blocking the aisle. Stumbling, she scattered the contents of her shopping bag over the floor along with the papers from the trash bin.

"Are you all right?" Corbin was by her side in an instant. "Let me help."

Rubbing her bruised shin, she frantically searched the deserted maze of cubicles. Where was the cleaning crew?

"I'm fine." Her cheeks heated. Even in a get-away, she was clumsy. "Just embarrassed."

They both crouched before the mess. Corbin sure was laying it on thick. His charm was clearly an affectation. Her first year out of graduate school, she'd fallen head over heels for the chief financial officer of the company she was auditing before she'd discovered his part in the fraud. He'd thought he could romance her away from turning over the evidence.

Sixteen months in federal prison had corrected his thinking.

Corbin shook his head. "Makes me crazy when people don't recycle."

"Should be a crime," Beth said, then cringed. If she didn't get ahold of herself, she'd wind up zipped in a body bag with a toe tag marked *murder by poisoning.* "Or not."

As she stuffed the papers back into the bin, her heart thumped against her ribs. She grasped her shopping bag and checked the contents. Nothing broken. Considering the price she'd paid for the small makeup compact this afternoon, she was grateful it had survived. The cosmetics were a treat to herself as she embarked on her temporary new life.

Her fingers brushed Corbin's arm, and she recoiled. She caught a hint of his spicy aftershave and held her breath. She'd always been a sucker for aftershave.

"Sorry," she mumbled.

"Not a problem."

What was wrong with her? She was Officer Greenwood's daughter, not a frightened extra in a horror movie. Even if Corbin was involved, he wasn't the person she needed to fear. As a cop's daughter, she had certain instincts about people. He didn't strike her as a cold-blooded killer.

Straightening, she brushed at her pencil skirt and eyed the exit at the far end of the aisle. Why had she worn sling-backs today? *Because today is just a normal day*, she reminded herself. She wasn't doing anything out of the ordinary that might draw attention to herself. Proper planning meant peak performance.

Clutching her leather bag against her chest, she backed away a few steps. "I'd better get going. Traffic."

"Let me walk you to your car."

"I'll be fine. This building is full of *security cameras*." She let the implication hang in the air between them. Every move she made left a cyber trail. Her gaze swung between the elevator door and the stairwell. She turned toward the stairs. "See you Monday."

"Tuesday," Corbin corrected. "Don't forget Monday is a federal holiday."

A flash of disappointment surprised her. She wouldn't be seeing him after today. Better she was leaving now before he directed the full, potent appeal of those ice-blue eyes on her. There was something about Corbin that had her feeling like a giggling schoolgirl with her first crush.

He adjusted his glasses on his nose. "I can't believe we get Columbus Day off. Any big plans for the holiday weekend?"

"Thought I'd organize my taxes."

"It's October."

"I work on a fiscal year." She cringed inwardly. "See you Tuesday."

"Enjoy your taxes." He quirked an eyebrow. "Don't worry. I can take a hint."

She opened and closed her mouth, then turned. If he was working for Cayman Holdings, he was an excellent undercover operative. If he was innocent, she'd just turned down her first chance at an actual date in over a year.

Who was she kidding?

He was up to something. There was no reason for him to zero in on her when Karli from marketing had been raising her hemlines and lowering her necklines since Corbin had taken up residence in the corner office.

Beth paused. Should she take the stairs? Corbin always took the stairs. They both did; that's how she knew his habits. *Don't deviate from the rou-*

tine. She wasn't any safer stuck with Corbin in the elevator than being alone with him in the stairwell. When she reached the end of the aisle, she glanced over her shoulder.

Corbin had disappeared.

A chill snaked down her spine. No one of his size should be able to disappear that quietly. Did they teach that sort of thing in Special Forces? Probably.

A new coffee house on Fifth Street. She snorted softly. She wasn't a complete fool.

Her heart racing, she took the stairs two at a time and pushed open the door to the parking garage. Only a couple other cars remained. Keeping her back straight and her gait purposeful, she crossed the distance.

The sound of her heels striking the concrete echoed through the cavernous, empty space. Pausing beside the car, she dug in her purse for her keys. Normally she kept them at the ready when exiting a parking garage. Corbin's unexpected appearance upstairs had distracted her.

As she fumbled with her purse, she dropped the bag. "Calm down, Beth."

She took a deep, relaxing breath. Everything was fine. She was overreacting. No one knew anything, least of all Corbin. Whatever suspicions he may have, she'd done nothing to confirm them.

Not yet. She scooped up her purse and stepped back. Glass crunched beneath her feet.

The hairs on the nape of her neck stirred, and she tipped back her head. The security camera hung from a single electrical wire. The glass lens was shattered.

A hand clamped over her mouth, stifling her scream.

Corbin raced down the stairs, the soles of his shoes squeaking over the tile surface.

He should be able to catch her. Petite and classily beautiful, Beth Greenwood's daily uniform consisted of a pencil skirt and blouse, her blond hair in a neat bun, and a sensible pair of pumps to complete the look. Not the best outfit for a speedy getaway.

Until now, her reputation had been impeccable, rendering his evidence circumstantial at best, but the coincidences were adding up. Her name had come up twice in connection to a fraudulent account. The first time she'd appeared on his radar, she'd switched jobs right in the middle of his investigation, and the trail had gone cold. She'd resurfaced yet again when she'd inquired about an offshore account he'd flagged for suspicious activity. Now it appeared as though she was going to perform another disappearing act before he could gather further evidence of her involvement.

Working on a hunch, he'd had her followed. Last week she'd deviated from her regular routine. She'd been seen with two men in a part of town known on the nightly news for drug deals gone bad. The pair of men she'd met in the seedy bar were known in the criminal underworld for helping people disappear. While Corbin couldn't prove she'd done anything but order a soda water, that meeting was too big a coincidence for a man who didn't believe in happenstance.

The train ticket protruding from her bag when she'd tripped over the trash bin had confirmed his suspicions. He'd tucked the revealing evidence deeper into the pocket before she'd noticed, but not before he'd memorized her departure. Tomorrow. 5:45 a.m. One way.

The accountant was running. Innocent people didn't run. She'd been his first suspect since her name had come up in the previous audit. Didn't help that she'd spent the past week behaving like a textbook example of a guilty person. She was edgy and jumpy—rarely leaving her desk—even for meals. She didn't want anyone messing with her computer. She didn't want anyone to know what she was doing. Innocent people had nothing to hide.

Strike one.

Corbin pushed open the door to the garage, and his blood froze.

A man had his arm clamped around Beth's waist, the other hand covering her mouth.

His adrenaline surged. She kicked and clawed. Her heels scuffed along the cement, and one of her shoes tumbled free. A car idled opposite the exit, a shadowy figure in the driver's seat, presumably the getaway vehicle. Ducking behind a pillar, Corbin rapidly scanned the garage. He'd backed his nondescript sedan into the spot opposite Beth's. The proximity was purposeful. If she was planning on disappearing, he wanted to know. He crouched and crossed the distance, then fished out his key fob and hit the button twice, remotely starting his car.

The man holding Beth spun toward the noise. The next instant he yelped and stumbled backward, clutching his face.

Beth held her arm extended, a canister of pepper spray in her outstretched hand. Writhing in pain, the man lurched away from her assault. He groped blindly in the direction of his waiting vehicle. Corbin dove into his car and slammed the transmission into First. He roared out of the space, positioning the passenger side before Beth.

Her face pale, she glanced up from her crouched position.

He leaned over the console and pushed open the door. "Get in!"

She scooped up her purse, her frightened gaze swinging between him and her car.

The pepper-sprayed man had reached the getaway vehicle. Still blinded, he fumbled with the handle.

Beth shook her head. "No."

"Get in!" he ordered. "There's no time."

A bullet ricocheted off the hood.

The getaway driver had a gun. The noise propelled her forward. She leaped into the passenger seat and slammed the door. Another bullet shattered the windshield of her car. Beth threw her arms over her face and crouched behind the dash.

Corbin shifted into Reverse and braced his hand on the back of the passenger seat. Looking over his shoulder, he sped down the garage ramp in reverse. When they reached the next level, he spun the wheel. The tires squealed and smoked, circling the car forward.

"Put on your seat belt," he ordered gruffly.

Her fingers fumbling, Beth complied. The parking-garage gate was open, and he raced through the exit. He didn't live in the city, but he'd gotten to know the layout over the past two weeks.

Glancing at the rearview mirror, he caught sight of the car following them. "Hang on. This might get bumpy."

He couldn't get a good look at the men driving. Average height and build. Sunglasses despite the cloudy sky. One of them was wearing a dark ball cap with lighter lettering. He squinted into the rearview mirror. Maybe a Bears hat. It was too difficult to discern.

The sky was overcast, creating an early twilight. He wove through the Friday afternoon traffic and turned on to a side street packed with orange cones and graded for resurfacing. He only needed a few twists and turns. The men following them were liable to give up easily. Traffic was heavy, and there were too many witnesses. A Friday evening in downtown Chicago meant extra police patrolling the tipsy happy-hour crowds.

He took a corner and then another. Cars filled in behind them, and he drove toward the freeway ramp. Soon they were caught in the rush of traffic. Concentrating on the road and keeping a watch for a tail kept his attention focused. Beth remained silent; her hands braced against the dash. He raised an eyebrow. Though she had her phone, she hadn't dialed the police. A cop's daughter who didn't call the police after an attack.

Strike two.

Once he was confident the men following them had given up, he exited the freeway and drove toward a park near his rented house. The lot was empty save for a single vehicle. A young couple played Frisbee in the distance, oblivious to the darkening sky.

He turned toward Beth and came face-to-face with her container of pepper spray.

Lifting his hands, he said, "Easy there. Don't shoot."

He'd been pepper-sprayed in the army, and he'd prefer not to repeat the experience.

"Who are you?" she demanded.

"Corbin Ross. You might remember me from the finance meeting this morning. The one with the stale donuts and the endless PowerPoint."

His joke lifted one edge of her mouth.

"Sam must have had over a hundred slides," she said.

"And half of them were charts."

Her blond hair had come loose from the severe bun she wore at the nape of her neck and tumbled over her shoulder in a gilded wave. Though her hands shook, she stared him down with a steely determination in her leaf-green eyes. Her words were light, but her intentions were deadly serious. His heartbeat kicked. This wasn't personal. This was business. The first rule of undercover work was *never get involved with your subject*. Fraternizing with a suspect was a surefire path to the unemployment line.

The container wavered. "Take me back to my car."

"I don't think that's a good idea," he said, soothingly. "Someone may be watching your car. Your apartment isn't safe, either. I'll take you to the police station."

"No." Her gaze narrowed. "No police."

"You can't run from this," he said. "Whatever you've done, it's time to own up."

A series of suspicious transactions with Cayman Holdings had brought Quetech Industries to the attention of the Cyber Division of Homeland Security. Two years before, Corbin had worked with the FBI on a case involving the same bank. A forensic accountant, Timothy Swan, had claimed to have evidence against Cayman Holdings, Limited. Beth Greenwood's name had come up during the investigation. With no suspects in Swan's death and insufficient evidence to pursue the fraud, the case had languished.

When the bank had come to the attention of Homeland Security once more, Corbin had volunteered for the undercover assignment. Beth Greenwood's employment at Quetech Industries had been too much of a coincidence. She'd worked with Timothy Swan before. She'd spoken to the accountant about the case before his death. This was the second time her name had been linked to Cayman Holdings.

For the past two weeks, Corbin had worn a suit and tie and gossiped over the water cooler. Two weeks hadn't given him enough time to unravel the complicated financial dealings. All he had were his suspicions, but they were adding up quickly.

"If you tell the truth," Corbin said. "I'll do what I can to help you."

He wasn't lying to her. Not exactly. As long as she turned over state's evidence, he'd put in a good word with the prosecutor.

"What are you saying?" Beth rapidly shook her head. "I didn't do anything wrong. Those men attacked *me*."

"What did they want?"

She ducked her head. "How should I know?"

"Then why aren't we going to the police station?"

Since he'd left the army for stateside government work, he'd seen plenty of embezzlement scandals. In his experience, white-collar criminals didn't hire killers when they were caught red-handed—they bought boats and disappeared in the Caribbean. Beth and Quetech Industries were involved in something far more sinister than simple embezzlement.

She shook her head. "It's complicated. The less you know, the better."

"Look, I'd rather be listening to Janice's rendition of 'Total Eclipse of the Sun' than having this conversation, but those men had guns. They used bullets."

One of them was embedded in the hood of his car. Evidence he'd check later.

The dark gray clouds overhead gave way, and a steady drumming of rain tapped against the car roof. The couple playing Frisbee dashed toward their vehicle, giggling and holding hands. The man held the Frisbee over the woman's head in a poor attempt to shield her from the rain.

Beth's distress tugged at Corbin, cementing his resolve. He had to keep his distance, both mentally and physically. He'd seen how her sort operated. Once she knew she was caught, there'd be a sob story, a tearful plea for clemency.

Except he wasn't in the business of providing sanctuary. "Do people just randomly kidnap you, or is this Friday special?"

The canister of pepper spray shook violently, and her breath came in quick, sharp gasps. "What about my car?"

As the shock penetrated her defenses, her bravado slipped.

"Your windshield is shot out. We caught them off guard. You're fortunate you weren't hit."

Her breath came in sharp huffs. She glanced through the rain-streaked windshield at the park, a frown puckering her forehead. "I can't just abandon my car."

"Breathe," he said. "They've probably stolen your car."

"Are you always this positive?"

"It's a gift."

Beth Greenwood didn't look like someone who'd launder money for terrorists, but what did he know? His midwestern childhood had been poor training for covert military ops. Everyone lied. Four years ago, his brother had trusted the wrong person, and that one mistake had cost his life. The loss had devastated their entire family. His sister-in-law and his nephew had suffered the worst. When Corbin had followed in his brother's footsteps and joined covert ops to settle the score, he'd kept the truth from his family. They'd been through too much already.

His parents didn't know what he did for a living now, or what he'd done in the army. They thought he was a desk jockey, and he let them believe the lie. He didn't want them to worry. After seeing what his sister-in-law was going through, raising a child alone, he'd known he had to choose between having a family and having this profession. He'd called off his engagement to his high school sweetheart. He'd chosen the job.

"I c-can't seem to stop s-shaking for some reason," Beth stuttered.

He tamped down a wave of sympathy for his frightened passenger. His personal life and his work life never mixed. Never. He existed in two different worlds. When he was with his family, the job didn't exist. When he was on the job, everyone else was an enemy. His ex had complained he kept too much hidden. She'd taken his secrecy personally. She'd never understood that it was all part of the job.

"It's the adrenaline." He slipped out of his jacket. "Take deep breaths and focus on a pleasant memory."

"Like what?" Beth asked. "I can't think of anything."

Her chest rose and fell in an uneven cadence. The sight of her bare foot, the painted toenails curled against the cold, tugged at something in his chest. She was going to hyperventilate soon.

"What was your favorite hobby as a kid?" he asked, an emotion he didn't want to identify spreading through him.

He didn't want to like her. He didn't want to feel sorry for her. This was a job, and in this job, the risk of betrayal was the difference between life and death.

"Horseback riding." She covered her mouth with her free hand, her words muffled. "I loved horseback riding."

She hesitated a moment before lowering the pepper spray. As she reluctantly accepted his coat, his fingers brushed against the silk of her blouse.

The rumble of the car engine and the steady patter of rain faded into the void.

"That's a good memory," he said. "Think about that."

"Sometimes we'd take drives on Sunday," Beth's voice grew quiet, and her eyes focused on something beyond the rain-dotted windshield. "I'd pretend I owned a horse, and my dad was taking me to the stables." Her breathing had slowed, and her vacant gaze drifted over him. "We didn't have the money. It was just a way of pretending. You know, how kids do sometimes?"

"Sure," he said. "What about your mother?"

"She died when I was six. Car accident. I don't remember much of her. Just impressions."

He'd only known Beth for two weeks, but he'd become familiar with her routine. He recognized the floral scent of her perfume and the steady cadence of her walk when she passed his office. He didn't know why she fascinated him, and he didn't like the feeling. Not one bit. Feelings had a way of making a person distracted and weak.

She wrapped her arms around her body and chafed her upper arms. "Take me back downtown."

"I live near here." He stalled. "I need to stop by my house. Then I'll take you anywhere you want to go."

There was a bullet hole in the hood of his car,

and the woman sitting next to him had become a liability to a terrorist cell laundering money. He didn't know the extent of her knowledge, and he wasn't letting her out of his sight.

She raised the canister once more. "All right. But I have the pepper spray, remember?"

"I'm not likely to forget." That stuff was potent. Residue had both their eyes watering in the confined space of the car. "I don't mean to be rude, but I did save your life. A simple 'thank you' would suffice."

He considered his original cover story. Considering the shock she'd had, he doubted she'd read too much into his earlier conversation. The less she knew at this point the better. He had a greater chance of inspiring her confidence if she didn't see him as a threat.

"I'm sorry." She ducked her head. "But I don't trust anyone from Quetech Industries right now."

"Why not?"

"I have my reasons." She swiped the back of her hand across her forehead. "Are you former military? I heard rumors."

"I served."

"I haven't done anything wrong. I promise you that."

"Sure." He blinked rapidly against the sting of the toxic spray. "Don't rub your eyes, it will only make them worse."

He shifted into gear and pulled out of the parking lot. His rental house sat at the end of a cul-de-sac populated by nondescript houses in a bedroom community. The previous occupants had been college kids, and his neighbors preferred having a quiet, single man next door instead of a noisy frat house. Keeping a low profile had been difficult with the welcoming bandwagon of visitors and casseroles.

He parked in the drive and left the engine running. He glanced at Beth's shivering frame and cranked the heater.

"I'll be right back," he said.

"Okay." Her complexion ashen, she clutched the passenger door handle as though she might leap out of the car at any moment. "Please don't take long."

She was terrified, that much of her story he believed. Were they blackmailing her? Somehow that was easier to swallow—picturing her as the innocent victim. What did it matter? That sort of thinking got people killed. He had a mission to accomplish. This wasn't the time to go soft.

"I'll be quick," he said.

A little time alone gave her a chance to stew over her present circumstances. Given the current technology, even if she stole his car, she wouldn't get far. Without transportation, she was at a considerable disadvantage. It was cold and raining, and she was in a strange neighborhood. There was no place to hide.

He took the shallow porch stairs two at a time and punched his security code into the panel. Once inside, he quickly unlocked his safe and retrieved his Glock. He strapped the holster around his shoulders.

Glancing outside, he caught sight of Beth's silhouette shimmering in the rain against the soft glow of the streetlight. If she finally decided to call the police, he'd deal with the interference. The police tended to be battering rams when he needed finesse, but at this point, he didn't have much choice.

Keeping vigil before the window, the lights doused to prevent glare, he retrieved his phone from his pocket and dialed a memorized number.

The voice on the other end answered with a curt, "What do you have?"

"A problem."

"Go ahead."

A pair of headlights flashed across the window. A vehicle pulled into the next driveway over, and Corbin squinted through the sheeting rain. He recognized his neighbor's familiar battered minivan with a parade of stick people marching across the back window.

"This is more than embezzlement," Corbin said. "Someone tried to grab the accountant in

the Quetech parking garage. They were professionals. Armed."

"Who?"

"I don't know." Corbin raked his hand through
his hair. "The civilian prevented an engagement."

"Then you were right about the terrorism connection."

"Looks that way."

"We'll see if they left any evidence behind in
the garage. Anything else?"

"Cayman Holdings isn't listed in Quetech's
public records, but I traced an email about the
bank."

"Where's the accountant now?"

"She's with me," Corbin said.

As long as she didn't bolt, she had a chance
at partial immunity. Maybe she hadn't meant
for things to go as far as they did. Maybe she
hadn't realized where the money was being fun-
neled. Maybe she wanted to repent. The Bible
said there'd be more joy in heaven for one sinner
who repented than for ninety-nine righteous men.

Or maybe he just wanted to make excuses for
her because he'd seen her hovering near the door
of the break room during the monthly celebra-
tion of birthdays and anniversaries. She'd lingered just beyond the crowd of coworkers as they
laughed and joked, looking in, but never crossing
the threshold.

He shook his head, clearing his thoughts, then turned and snatched his identification from the open safe.

None of that mattered. She was in his custody, whether she knew it or not. She was suspicious of him, a disadvantage. Right now, she was probably weighing her options. Trying to decide if she was more afraid of him, the police, or the men in the garage.

Given that he didn't trust her allegiance, he wasn't confident how she'd react to his true identity.

Another pair of headlights flashed across the front window. The hazy shape of another car snagged his attention. His neighbor, Ruth, and her husband drove a sedan, but he couldn't decipher the make and model from this distance through the rain-streaked window.

"You still there?" the voice on the other end of the line demanded.

Corbin stepped closer, and his breath fogged the glass. "The accountant needs protective custody."

"I can't authorize the expense until we know for certain she has viable information."

"She's become a liability. Those men weren't taking her out for ice cream."

"I trust your judgment, but I need something concrete. Find out what she knows. I'll walk this up the chain and see what I can do."

A car door slammed.

Corbin's scalp tingled. "We'll talk later."

He raced out of the house and skidded to a halt. His driver's door hung open, and his jacket lay neatly folded on the seat. Rain trickled down his collar, and he muttered an oath.

Beth hadn't called the police. She'd run. *Strike Three.*

TWO

Beth cut through several yards, grateful for the chain-link fences and caring pet owners who kept their guard dogs safe by the fire when it rained. Ominous clouds blocked the setting sun, rapidly darkening the twilight. Enormous trees dotted the landscape of older homes. Above her, leaves in brilliant shades of autumnal gold and crimson remained caught in that stunning moment before the branches grew bare for winter. The wind whipped between the close-set houses, turning the chilled rain into icy, stinging pellets.

Her heels sank in the rain-soaked grass. At least she'd had the presence of mind to grab her shoe in the parking garage. She spotted the glowing lights of a gas station in the distance and traversed a low retaining wall into an alley behind a row of houses. She dodged between garbage cans and detached garages, making her way toward the streetlights at the far end of the block.

Who was Corbin Ross?

One thing was obvious—he was no financial consultant. He'd handled the terrifying situation in the parking garage with far too much aplomb. He'd also known she lived in an apartment. A lucky guess? Maybe. He'd said he'd served in the military, but he hadn't elaborated. Had he been with Special Forces? Was he a mercenary?

He could be working for the Feds, for Quetech Industries or for Cayman Holdings Limited. None of which boded well for her.

Huddled beneath the awning of the nearby gas station and tucked in the shadows, she ordered an Uber. For the next fifteen minutes, she danced from foot to foot and rubbed her hands together in an awkward dance to keep warm.

She'd collided with Corbin moments after hitting Send. What had he seen? At the very least, he'd lied to her. He certainly wasn't a financial officer living in the suburbs. Corbin might have saved her life, but he hadn't earned her trust. Whatever his loyalties, he was hiding something.

With each passing set of headlights, she searched for his car. Would he try and follow her? If he was with the Feds, would he call the police?

From what she'd learned from her dad, the Feds didn't call in the local police unless they were desperate. They thought cops leaked information like sieves, and they were overly cautious with their loyalties. A fact that might work to her advantage depending on Corbin's true identity. She didn't want the world; she only wanted to survive until tomorrow.

Keeping out of sight, she followed the driver's progress on her phone app and only stepped from her cover when the car pulled beneath the lighted awning.

The Uber driver barely blinked at her unkempt state. Beth mumbled "Union Station" and collapsed on to the worn upholstery.

Once at the train station, she hunched her shoulders and ducked her head, keeping her gaze averted from the ever-present cameras. An overweight security guard wearing an ill-fitting uniform gazed at her from his post. She flashed a smile, and her stomach clenched. How did criminals manage? Appearing innocent while terrified was harder than it seemed and infinitely more exhausting.

She checked the time on her phone, and her pulse picked up rhythm. She'd left Corbin's house forty-five minutes ago. Time was ticking away. Earlier that week, she'd made a shorter trip from this same station, and had purposefully left her luggage behind on the train. Ensuring the porter found it before a thief had been tricky, but not impossible. She retrieved her backpack from the unclaimed luggage department and ducked into the bathroom.

A harried mother ushered a crying toddler into the stall beside her. As Beth changed, the hassled mother spoke with false cheerfulness to the sobbing child about their impending vacation. An announcement for the next train came over the PA system.

The mother breathed a sigh. "See? That's our train. An hour late for delays and repairs. If you're good on the trip, I'll let you play Super Why on the iPad."

The allure of digital distraction appeased the toddler more than the promise of a lengthy, dull train ride. Beth waited until they left the restroom before she exited the stall.

She stuffed her clothing in the trash and stared into the mirror. The face looking back at her was pale and drawn, a fitting match for the ball cap, hoodie and jeans she'd donned.

The PA announced the imminent departure of the next train once more, and she tugged her lower lip between her teeth.

For the past month, she'd been in training for her new identity. The instructions from her dad's former informants when she'd arranged for her false identity had been specific and succinct: *Think about your disappearance at least as much as you thought about what put you on the run in the first place.*

She crossed the vaulted lobby and froze. A man

in a suit was speaking with the uniformed security guard. He flashed identification.

Pivoting on her heel, she ducked behind an automated kiosk, then peered around the edge. The man tucked his badge into his breast pocket, and she sucked in a breath. There was no reason to assume the man was here for her. Corbin didn't know how she was escaping the city. She tamped down her twinge of guilt. Even if he was with the Feds, she'd turned over all the evidence she had.

She shouldn't have to die, as well.

The security guard motioned the suited man toward the restroom, and she spun around. They passed beside her, and she carefully circled the kiosk. Once both men were out of sight, she approached the counter and exchanged her ticket. She'd initially planned on heading south on the California Zephyr in the morning, but the unexpected attack in the garage had forced a change in her itinerary. If someone had been keeping a watch on her, she'd best alter her original route. The attendant grumbled but eventually agreed if she paid an extra fee.

Fifteen minutes later she took her seat in a roomette on the Empire Builder train. Her heel tapped against the floor, and she glanced over her shoulder. Loading the train took an eternity, and she peered out the window on to the platform. The excursion was crowded, filled with families and vacationers, but nothing suspicious caught her attention.

The harried family with the upset toddler struggled their way down the narrow aisle in a squall of luggage, cheerful promises of the fabulous trip ahead, and the faint odor of apple juice.

Beth shut the door and tugged the curtains over the square window of her private roomette—a tiny space featuring two facing seats and an overhead bunk that pulled down. The wheels finally chugged, and the train lurched. She exhaled her pent-up breath. As the station faded into the distance, her pulse gradually slowed to a normal rhythm.

An hour into the trip, she almost felt as though she could breathe normally again.

A knock on the door sent her heart leaping into her throat.

"Yes?" she asked, her voice strangled.

"Complimentary beverage and snack service."

She hesitated, then realized she hadn't eaten since lunch. Her stomach rumbled. She stood and opened the door.

Corbin Ross stared back at her. "Going someplace?"

She attempted to slam the door, and he blocked the move with his foot. "We need to talk."

Corbin crowded into the tiny room and closed the pocket door. "Your destination is Portland, I believe. Plenty of time to tell me everything you know about Quetech Industries."

He'd sat in the lounge car for the past hour sipping water and gathering information as the scenery chugged by the window. Beth had the means and opportunity for the money laundering, but the motive remained frustratingly elusive. People did not operate randomly. Greed and revenge covered most crimes. Though some criminals merely liked to watch the world burn, she didn't seem the type.

She glanced behind him. "Does this mean I don't get a snack?"

At the defeated look on her face, he almost felt sorry for her. Almost. "Not complimentary."

Beth slumped on to a chair, and he took the opposite seat. He'd never seen the accountant dressed casually. Wearing a ball cap and jeans with her face scrubbed of makeup, she appeared younger and more vulnerable. His focus slipped, and he steeled his resolve. This wasn't personal. This was the job. Losing his concentration had the potential to cost lives.

"How did you find me so quickly?" she asked, her expression wan and defeated.

The terror alert was high during the holiday weekend, which meant there was a field agent at Union Station. Corbin had put out a watch for Beth, but her change of plans had caught him off guard.

He'd nearly missed the train. "My keen powers of intellect and deduction."

She raised an eyebrow.

"I caught a break."

"Are you with the FBI?"

"Homeland Security." He retrieved his identification from his pocket. "Cyber Division."

She snorted. "That figures."

"Don't you want to check up on me? You should be more careful. I might have forged this identification."

"At first I thought you might be a mercenary. Except no self-respecting thug would wear his hair cut that way."

"I was undercover." He ran his fingers through the close-clopped strands. "Defeats the purpose if I look like a thug."

He'd been out of the military for two years; maybe it was time to change barbers.

"I bet." She set her chin in a stubborn line. "I have nothing to say."

"I don't believe you." A muscle ticked along his temple. She was out to save her own hide, which made her both desperate and dangerous. "The truth will set you free. Eventually. Federal prison isn't that bad."

"I'm not upset because I'm going to federal prison," she spoke through clenched teeth. "I'm upset because I'm going to die."

"Relax." He took off his dark-rimmed glasses and polished the rain-smudged lenses on his sleeve. "You've been reading too many spy novels. I'm not going to kill you, Beth."

"I'm not worried about you." She leaned forward and clutched her head. "I can't believe I didn't even make it out of the city."

Given the fate of the last accountant who'd tangled with Cayman Holdings, she had good reason to be afraid.

"Tell me." He replaced his glasses. "How much does it cost to disappear these days?"

Her gaze remained fixed on the toes of her pristine sneakers. "I wouldn't know."

The shoes were new. The brim of her baseball cap was stiff and unbent. She'd planned her escape in advance. While he had to admire her careful preparation, something she'd done had tipped off the men in the garage.

"You're lying," he said. She hadn't purchased this ticket under the name Beth Greenwood. "I'm curious. How does an accountant find the sort of men who deal in false identities?"

"Forensic accountant." She corrected. "I'm a forensic accountant."

"There's a difference?"

"About twenty-thousand dollars' in student loans."

"You don't have any student loans."

Her head shot up. "How long have you been investigating me?"

"Long enough," he said. "You left two jobs precipitously. I know why you left Quetech, but why did you leave your first job out of graduate school?"

"Oldest story in the book. A relationship gone wrong."

"That's not what your file says."

Her mouth opened and closed. "What does my file say?"

"You should know better than me."

He schooled his features to remain impassive. Beth Greenwood was an enigma. She was twenty-eight years old, and she'd earned a bachelor's degree and an MBA from Georgetown. Her father had been a Chicago policeman. She was single and lived alone. Her credit rating was excellent, and she carried zero debt. She didn't have a car loan, a mortgage or even a student loan payment. She didn't have pets. Not a dog, not a cat, not a fish. She'd spent more days in hotels the previous year than she had in her apartment.

Her current circumstances bore an eerie resemblance to his own. He ran a finger beneath his collar. He hadn't had time to change, which meant he was still wearing his suit from work. Beth had worn his suit jacket in the car, and her floral scent lingered in the lining.

A lot of people traveled for work. Not everyone owned a pet.

She glared at him. "Am I under arrest or something?"

"Not yet."

"Then I have nothing to say." She crossed her arms over her chest. "And I'd like you to leave. This roomette is private."

And tiny. They sat face-to-face on seats that pushed together to transform the room into a sleeper car. Their knees practically touched. Outside the tinted window, lights darted past in the twilight. Beth grimaced and flipped shut the curtains. He tapped his index finger against his knee. She wasn't wholly alarmed by him if she'd closed the curtain against onlookers. A good indicator that he could negotiate her cooperation.

"What do you know about Cayman Holdings?" he asked.

Her complexion paled. "Nothing."

"Those men didn't try and kill you for nothing." His gaze narrowed. "You're terrified for a reason."

"If I'm not under arrest, then I'm not obligated to speak with you." She pursed her lips and stared at the curtained window. "That's all I'm saying."

"Your dad was a cop, Beth. You know how this works." Corbin had no choice but to appeal to her conscience. "This is bigger than you and me."

"I did what I could to help."

His stomach growled, and he checked the time on his phone. "Let's get something to eat. I'm hungry."

No need to rush her. There was nowhere to run on a moving train, and he doubted they'd been followed this far. Beth had purchased her ticket at the last minute, and no other passengers had booked travel after he boarded. Her attackers were probably sitting vigil outside her Chicago apartment.

Her gaze flicked toward him. "If you knew where I was, why didn't you question me before we left Chicago? Wouldn't that have been easier?"

"No time." He'd counted on her having the information with her. Why run unless she had insurance? Minneapolis was the nearest field office large enough to handle the assignment. "The train was an unexpected detour, I'll grant you that."

"That's why I chose it," she said. "I still don't know how you found me so quickly."

"Trade secret."

If she hadn't tripped over the garbage bin, he'd be chasing his tail around the airports and car rentals.

Beth rubbed a weary hand over her eyes, and his emotions softened. No matter her connection to the men who'd tried to grab her earlier this evening, she'd had a shock, and she was still recovering. If he was going to gather information, he had to go easy. Patience wasn't exactly his strongest virtue, but they had plenty of time to kill.

He stood. "C'mon. I'll buy you dinner."

She hesitated before nodding. "All right. But only because I'm starving, and you're buying."

"Excellent. We're making progress already."

"I have a feeling I'll pay for this free meal later."

"Spoken like a true accountant." He held up his hands. "Forensic accountant."

His correction earned a reluctant smile. He quickly glanced away.

They made their way down the cramped aisles. Forced to walk single file, his hand hovered near the small of her back in an unconsciously proprietary gesture. Upon reaching the dining car, they claimed an empty booth. The windows domed over them, the passing lights sparkling through the beaded rain. The setting might have been romantic save for the circumstances.

His phone buzzed, and he frowned at the number. "You mind if I take this?"

"Go ahead." She rolled her eyes. "Like you care what I think."

The rebuke stung more than it should have. He'd been raised on the Golden Rule. Some part of him always wanted to believe in the inherent goodness in people, and that part was going to get him killed someday if he wasn't more careful.

"Mr. Ross?" the elderly female voice on the other end spoke.

"Yes."

"This is your neighbor, Ruth. Remember I brought you dinner when you moved in?"

"Yes. I remember." He had three others in the freezer. For reasons he couldn't explain, married women believed that single men were perpetually in dire need of lasagna. "It was delicious. How can I help you, Ruth?"

"You know I don't like to pry, but you said I could call you anytime."

"Absolutely." He lifted his eyes heavenward. "Anytime."

"There's a strange car parked in your drive, but no lights on inside. I thought I saw the beam from a flashlight. I can't tell with all this rain. But something seems suspicious."

A flicker of apprehension sharpened his focus. "What kind of car?"

"You know, a car. Four doors…"

That narrowed it down. If his house was being searched, the intruder hadn't tripped his alarm. He'd have been notified by now.

"Are there any other cars parked on the street?" he asked.

He'd fielded more than one late-night encounter with a drunken college kid looking for a party who hadn't gotten word the frat boys had moved.

"Let me check," Ruth said.

A lengthy pause followed. The waitress appeared at their table. Following Beth's order of a chicken salad croissant, Corbin angled his phone away and requested a club sandwich.

"I'm back." Ruth declared. "Just the car in your drive."

"I'll take care of it, Ruth."

"Would you like me to call the police?" she asked, a trill of hope in her request. "I can hang up with you and call them right now."

"It's, uh, probably my girlfriend," Corbin assured her. He didn't need an unsuspecting officer stumbling into this mess. "She's watering the plants while I'm out of town. I appreciate the call. If you see anything else out of the ordinary, let me know. Talk soon." He disconnected the call before she could continue the conversation.

Beth glanced up from her glass of water. "Everything all right?"

"Not exactly."

He rested the phone on the table and stared out the window. There was no way the men from the parking garage had discovered his identity. The address listed on his car registration and his Quetech Industries employee paperwork didn't match where he currently lived. They hadn't followed him, or he'd have seen their car.

Beth tilted her head. "What is it?"

If they hadn't traced him, then they must be tracking Beth. But how? Or had she deliberately given someone his address?

His determination hardened. Beth Greenwood had worked with Timothy Swan on the Cayman Holdings case. She had information she wasn't sharing. She was running. She'd get them both killed if he didn't stay on his guard.

He had to assume the worst—that she was a knowing accomplice to a money-laundering scheme that was funding a sleeper terrorist cell. At the very least, she must be profiting. Why else would she be involved?

His lips twisted in a cynical smile. "Give me your phone."

THREE

Beth instinctively covered her pocket. "Why do you want my phone?"

"That was my neighbor," Corbin said. "There's a chance the men from the garage are at my house."

"Oh." Wading into his personal life muddled her thoughts. "You said your girlfriend was there."

She didn't want to think of him as a regular person with a family and mundane responsibilities. He was standing in the way of her successful escape. Not the sort of relationship she needed in her life right now. Despite the fact she was drawn to him. Had a crush on him. No, she was just attracted to him. Who wouldn't be? She was only human, after all. He was cute and funny when he wasn't questioning her like a suspect.

"I don't have a girlfriend," he said.

She tamped down her flare of relief. It didn't matter that Corbin didn't have a girlfriend. His personal life was of absolutely no interest to her. She was merely relieved he was working with the government and not Cayman Holdings. She'd live longer that way. Maybe not much longer, but at least she had a few more days. Or hours.

"Why don't you call the police?" she grumbled.

"I'd rather not involve local law enforcement."

"You government types are all the same." She snorted. "The police might be able to help."

"Or they might get hurt. There's nothing at my house worth stealing. They won't find anything revealing, and I'm not risking the life of an officer over my toothbrush."

Her stomach dipped. "I didn't think of that."

She'd seen Corbin pretending to be a staid and steady financial consultant, and she'd seen him handle himself with chilling ease when the bullets were flying. She'd yet to see this side of him. The lazy cordiality he'd shown before had disappeared, and his focus was razor sharp. Though his demand to see her phone annoyed her, she didn't see the harm in letting him look. She had nothing to hide. At least not in this regard.

"Did you call anyone?" he asked.

"An Uber. That was all. This is a new phone and a new number."

"Did you really think no one would notice if Beth Greenwood disappeared?"

"Arranging the disappearance of Beth Greenwood was the easiest part of the plan," she mumbled. "No one pays much attention to temporary employees."

"I did."

"Only because you suspected me of laundering money for a crime syndicate."

Something flickered in his gaze. "Crime syndicate?"

"Yeah. Isn't that what this is all about?"

Working freelance around the country twenty days a month didn't leave much time for socializing. She didn't even have a cat. She had a few friends, but given her work, they often went weeks without speaking. She'd turned down so many invitations to lunch, people had ceased asking.

"You didn't call anyone else?" he prodded. "No family? No friends?"

"No one," she said, a defensive edge in her answer.

There was no one to call.

A twinge of regret speared through her. When had everything tethering her to mundane social interactions disappeared? She'd made excuses for not keeping in touch. Nobody talked on the phone anymore, and she'd given up on social media. Her Facebook account had languished for months. Cute kittens had morphed into endless baby photos which had subsequently transitioned into political rants. There was no reason to scroll through the boundless pages of happy family photos and competing politics.

Corbin slid the backs of his knuckles across

the table and flexed his fingers. "Who else has this number?"

"Nobody."

Since her dad's death, she wasn't listed as the emergency contact on any forms. By the time anyone became suspicious of her disappearance, she'd counted on the FBI clearing the case, and that's when she'd quietly resurrected Beth Greenwood. She'd planned on a few weeks, possibly a month. No one would be suspicious until maybe the holidays when folks started looking for excuses to get together.

"I still need to check," he said. "This is important. If they're tracking us, I need to know how. Like it or not, judging by the attack in the parking garage, Beth Greenwood left a trail before she disappeared."

The censure in his voice raised her hackles. "You're awful judgmental for a man who fakes his identity for a living."

"What I do is legally sanctioned by the government. Can you make the same claim?"

"This was a matter of life and death. Doesn't that count for immunity?"

"You should have asked for help."

"And the serpent said unto the woman," Beth quoted the Bible beneath her breath, *"Ye shall not surely die."*

"What was that?"

"Nothing."

The only guilt she felt was for not caring more about her deception. Letting go of Beth Greenwood had filled her with a curious sense of relief. She had a fresh start and a clean slate. She wasn't the person who'd gotten Timothy killed. She hadn't fallen for the first embezzler in a suit who'd shown her a scrap of attention after emerging from the haze of caring for her dad. She didn't have to endure another audit as a hostile presence among her temporary coworkers.

While she loved her job, she hadn't anticipated the isolation that accompanied fraud investigations. Even innocent people were chilled by her presence.

"Fine," she said. "You can check my phone. But you won't find anything."

After she typed in the security code, she handed it over. He didn't trust her. She wasn't a complete idiot—he was investigating her more than looking for a tracking device. Not that she blamed him. Neither of them had much reason to trust the other.

"What about *your* phone?" she demanded. "Who did you contact?"

Corbin flipped through her call history, turned the case over and removed the back cover. "My phone is encrypted and untraceable."

"Are you certain? Maybe someone did a background check on you," she scoffed. "The office rumor is that you were Special Forces in the military."

His head snapped up. "Who started that rumor?"

"Someone who saw the tattoo on your arm."

She'd like to get a look at that ink. *No.* She didn't want to see his tattoos or hear about his family or listen to him talk with his neighbor. He wasn't the enemy, but he wasn't an ally, either. They were at cross purposes. He wanted evidence against Cayman Holdings, and she wanted to live. Near as she could tell, those two goals were mutually exclusive.

"Huh." He continued his search of her phone. "I can't believe anyone at Quetech Industries was that observant. Half the people couldn't even get my name right. They kept calling me Clark. Even you."

A flush spread across her cheeks. "That's because your nickname is Clark. You know, like the mild-mannered reporter from film and television fame."

"The one who turns into a superhero?"

"Yeah. Because of, you know, the glasses."

He sat back in his seat. "You're right. Must be the specs."

The glasses, the piercing blue eyes, the way he'd jog up eight flights of stairs without getting winded. That time he'd carried two five-gallon jugs for the water cooler on his broad shoulders. His chiseled jaw.

But let him believe it was the eyewear. "Mmm-hmm."

"There's nothing here," he said, glancing at her backpack. "What else did you take with you from home?"

"Nothing. I dumped my clothes and my purse at the train station. Everything here is new."

She'd even bought new makeup that afternoon. Being pampered at the department store makeup counter was one of her few indulgences. Some people drank. Some people ate chocolate. She purchased expensive cosmetics. Not the best method of coping, but not the worst, either.

"Discernably new," he said. "Let me see your hat."

Too confused to argue, she handed it over.

He bent the brim and scooted it back across the table. "That's better."

The waitress delivered their food, and they both fell silent. They went through the familiar, comforting rituals of arranging silverware, glasses and napkins. Famished, she dug into her meal. She'd been too nervous to eat much the past few days.

Corbin sliced through his sandwich. "If they had a tracer in your bag, and you switched in Chicago, they'd only get as far as Union Station. There are plenty of routes leaving from there, which should slow them down. That might buy us some time."

"You're still assuming it's me. You worked for Quetech Industries. You were a new hire. Maybe they suspected you were spying. I certainly did."

"You did?" His knife and fork stalled over his plate. "Why?"

"Because you asked me out on a date, that's why." Humiliation burned through her chest. "People worried about getting caught for laundering money approach the forensic accountant first. It's like a game. They always think they're smart enough to fool us, and they're always wrong."

"Is it so strange that I'd ask you on a date?"

"Karaoke? Really?"

"Maybe I was curious about Janice's singing voice." He had the decency to appear abashed. "You want to talk about Timothy Swan?"

Her stomach knotted, and she set down her sandwich. "He's the reason I'm trying to disappear."

Timothy had been a good man. A kind mentor who was worried about her safety when he should have been looking out for himself.

"You need my help," Corbin said. "They're obviously on to you."

"Maybe." She swiped at her mouth, as though she could erase the memory of the man's hand clamped painfully over her lips. "I can't figure out how. I was extremely careful."

"Homeland Security and the FBI will protect you."

"Like they protected Timothy Swan?"

Corbin made a sound of frustration. "Tell me more about your relationship with him."

She studied his expression for signs of deception, but he appeared genuinely curious. "Timothy was a mentor. I worked with him my first year out of college. He helped me through a difficult time. We became friends. He'd lost his wife. I'd lost my dad. I was the daughter he never had, and he was like a surrogate dad. We understood each other. Two years ago, I was working with a small conglomerate in Houston, and something stirred my suspicions."

Corbin tilted his head. "What?"

"Instinct, I guess. Why does a company that sells copiers need an offshore account? How were they doing millions of dollars of business out of a strip mall? I asked for Timothy's help deciphering some usual transactions I'd tracked through Cayman Holdings. He insisted on taking the evidence to the FBI himself."

She paused, her throat working.

Corbin drummed his fingers on the table. "Didn't you think that was unusual? Why not advise you to contact the authorities yourself?"

"Because he was protective of me." She pressed her thumb and forefinger against her eyelids and pictured Timothy's reading glasses perched on the edge of his nose. She saw the ink on his jacket sleeves, smeared from his favorite fountain pen. He'd been a throwback to another generation. "This community is tight-knit. He'd heard rumors the bank was involved with the Russian mafia." Pressure built behind her eyes. "You know what happened next."

"He was poisoned." Corbin's expression didn't flicker. "Poisoning is modus operandi for the Russians."

"Then the rumors were true?"

"I don't know. The case is still open under FBI jurisdiction, but there hasn't been any progress."

Beth choked back a sob. Poisonings happened in TV detective shows and movies. She never thought she'd be tangled in an international web of deceit.

She was an *accountant*, after all. "I didn't know someone was still investigating his death. I thought they'd forgotten about him." She'd followed the case, but there were no leads. No suspects. Only suspicions. While she was grateful someone was interested in discovering the truth of Timothy's death, something didn't quite fit. "What does Homeland Security want with a foreign mafia? Especially if the FBI has jurisdiction over the case."

"Cybersecurity covers all sorts of interference."

"Now you sound evasive."

"I'm being as honest as I can be considering the situation."

Which was simply another way of saying he didn't trust her.

Her thoughts drifted back to her last conversation with Timothy. He'd been her mentor during her first internship, and they'd remained friends long after she'd graduated.

"I never should have gone to Timothy." She pushed away her plate, her gaze growing blurry. "If I hadn't confided in him, he'd still be alive. I never imagined… I was naive. I suppose I just never…"

"Don't think like that." Corbin reached across the table before quickly retracting his hand. His expression shifted, and he dropped his arm to his side. "It wasn't your responsibility to protect Timothy Swan."

"Then whose was it?"

He took a deep breath, his nostrils flaring. "Mine."

She narrowed her gaze. "I don't understand."

"Why do you think I'm here, Beth?" For the first time since she'd met him two weeks ago, there was a weary, almost defeated note in his voice. "The FBI brought Timothy's information to the Cyber Division of Homeland Security. That was my case. My responsibility."

"You?" The full implication of his words seeped through the fog of her shock, and the space closed in around her. She felt as though someone had dropped a weight on her chest. "Then you met him?"

"We had an initial meeting. There was nothing solid in the evidence, but there was enough to connect the dots. I requested protective custody, but the request was denied."

She gripped her hands in her lap to stop the trembling. "Why?"

Clearly Timothy had been in danger.

"I was working on a hunch, and I was new to the division." The set of Corbin's jaw grew rigid. "His death was my mistake. I should have pressed harder. I've been waiting two years for another chance at Cayman Holdings."

"I've been a gullible idiot, haven't I?" She hung her head and rubbed her fingers against her forehead, pressing the tips over her deepening worry lines. "Have you been tracking me the entire time?"

"No. You weren't considered a suspect. Timothy kept your name out of the initial inquiry. Following his death, we investigated his contacts. His friends. That made you notable, but not a suspect."

She didn't entirely believe his answers, and she'd learned to trust her instincts over the years. Sometimes the tip-off wasn't the mistake, the tip-off was when the columns balanced the first time perfectly. Honest people made mistakes. Crooks went overboard to make everything look flawless. A lack of errors often meant that someone was trying too hard.

Considering Timothy's fate, even with the protection of Homeland Security, the chances of her surviving this ordeal had dropped by at least fifty percent.

Her chicken salad sandwich sat like a rock in her stomach. "What happens now?"

"There's an FBI field office in Minneapolis. I need to know everything you've uncovered regarding Quetech Industries."

A tiny flame of hope ignited within her. "Then you believe I'm innocent?"

"We'll know soon enough."

The tiny flame sputtered and died. "I have an impeccable reputation. That should count for something."

"You were running, Beth," he said. "Under an assumed name. What am I supposed to think? In my line of work, actions speak louder than words."

Despite the warmth of the dining car, she shivered. The evidence she'd sent to the FBI this evening took on an even greater importance. She wasn't simply being morally courageous by turning over what she knew; that email might be the key to keeping herself out of prison.

She fiddled with the edge of her plate. "Quetech was laundering money for Cayman Holdings through several shell accounts. The system was ingenious. I would never have caught the transactions if I hadn't seen something similar two years before. They'd changed the name of the shell corporation, but the address was the same. An empty office in an industrial park."

"You remembered an address two years after the fact?"

"The name of the street was my middle name, and it just stuck in my head."

He reached into his breast pocket and retrieved a small notebook and a pen. "Then working at Quetech was just a coincidence?"

He jotted down a few notes, and she pictured Timothy's ink-stained sleeves. Pen and paper. A throwback to another generation.

"An awful coincidence," she said. "As soon as I saw the name, I should have walked away. But I couldn't. Timothy was dead because I hadn't acted before." Her dad had never backed down from a dangerous choice, and she couldn't disappoint him. "I owed it to him to see this through."

"You never considered catching a little action

of your own? You could have gotten paid a lot of money to look the other way."

"For what shall it profit a man, if he shall gain the whole world, and lose his own soul?"

"Mark 8:36." He grunted. "Yeah. I went to Bible school, too. Do you have any proof of these transactions?"

"I sent an email with everything the FBI needs to trace the payments to the Chicago field office. It's time-stamped for delayed delivery. It'll be there first thing Tuesday morning after the holiday. Everything you need is in that email."

His pen skipped over the page. "To a general account, or did you address the email to someone specific?"

"An agent named Stephen Keel. Timothy had worked with him before."

Corbin glanced up. "Do you have access to the information now?"

"No."

The pen stilled. "Where is it?"

"I sent a list of the transactions and the monetary amounts from a private email account and used the Quetech computer."

"Can you recreate it from memory?"

"Some. Not all. There are account numbers. I can't remember them all. Without those numbers, you'll be looking for a needle in a haystack."

"You sent the email from a work computer."

He tapped his pen against the notebook. "Which means any ghosted information is still at Quetech." He jotted another note. "Why not simply walk out with the information on a flash drive?"

"Because I needed to buy some time. I didn't want anyone to track me. If I left the ghosted information on my home computer, there'd be a trace. If I had the files on a flash drive and they caught me, I'd have no insurance. They'd take the drive and kill me."

"You needed the delay to catch a train and assume a new identity." He lifted an eyebrow. "They found you, anyway. How?"

She threw up her hands. "I don't know. I was careful. At least I thought I was."

Not careful enough. Corbin had been on to her from the beginning, after all. Then again, for all she knew, he'd been tracking her for the past two years. Either way, the case against her didn't look good. She'd been linked to Cayman Holdings on two occasions. She'd purchased a false identity from a couple of her dad's former informants, and she'd attempted to disappear. Everything pointed to her guilt.

Corbin retrieved his phone and typed something. "What about the account you used to send the email? There should be a copy in the Sent folder."

"I'm not a complete idiot." She rolled her eyes.

"I didn't use a regular email account. I used an encrypted service called No Going Back. The emails are time stamped."

"A private service?" He grimaced. "Can you access the information?"

"No. That's the whole point. Once the email is time stamped for delivery, there's *no going back*. According to the website, it's primarily used for relationship breakups and deathbed confessions. I needed a delay that was untraceable."

The idea had seemed inspired at the time, giving her a chance to run. Except now she had no way to prove her innocence until the email was delivered. As it stood, she could just as easily be covering her tracks as turning over relevant information. Her fraudulent identity made the optics appear even worse. Three days suddenly seemed like a very long time.

"You're telling me people send deathbed messages before they die." Corbin rested his elbow on the table and splayed his hands. "That doesn't make any sense. How is someone supposed to know when they're going to die?"

"The system emails the sender at predesignated intervals. If you don't reply with a receipt of confirmation, they assume you're deceased and automatically send the correspondence."

He rolled his eyes. "There's no possible way

that can ever go wrong." Corbin pushed her plate closer to her. "Eat."

"I'm not hungry."

"You'll feel better if you eat something," he said, a softness in his voice she hadn't heard before. "Try."

"I know my situation doesn't look good." She plucked at the lettuce edging her sandwich. "I needed a few days to disappear. I needed a way to send the information from Quetech without leaving an obvious trail. I knew they'd find out about me sooner or later, but I was counting on *later* in order to survive."

"Then you should have contacted the authorities."

"That didn't work out too well for Timothy."

"We don't know who killed Timothy. We don't know who else he was involved with."

Her lips pursed, she clenched her fists. "Don't you dare say anything against Timothy. He was a good man. An honest man. He didn't have to protect me, but he did, and it cost him his life. He had a family. People who loved him. He doesn't deserve someone like you questioning his integrity."

If she didn't know better, she'd have thought guilt flitted across his features. "I'm not questioning your friend's integrity, but I have to examine all the possibilities."

She pressed her fist against her mouth. He

didn't care about Timothy any more than he cared about her. She was a means to end, not a person. Taking a deep breath, she lowered her hand.

"What now?" she asked.

"We wait until Tuesday," Corbin said. "And we ensure your email arrives safe and sound. I'd rather have the information now, but we'd need a warrant." He scrolled through the screens on his phone, then typed something with his thumbs. "It appears that No Going Back is located offshore. Without jurisdiction, a warrant takes even longer. Which means we lay low and wait for your initial email. If the information is sound, we'll protect you."

"You can't hold me." Panic straightened her vertebrae. "You can't prove I've done anything wrong."

His expression turned grim, and her stomach dropped.

"In cases of terrorism, the department is allotted a generous amount of leeway."

Her vision swam. "Terrorism?"

"I will do whatever I have to do to prevent another Boston Marathon."

"I didn't know…" She'd have handled everything differently. She'd thought she was dealing with a drug runner, not a terrorist. Her head throbbed. It was too late now. "I'll do whatever I can to help."

"Yes. You will." Corbin offered a smile that didn't quite reach his eyes. "And for the next three days, you and I are going to be inseparable."

Her shoulders slumped. She'd tried, and she'd failed. That email was supposed to be her insurance, not her death sentence.

Just past midnight, Corbin knocked on Beth's roomette. The FBI had balked at taking jurisdiction of Beth until they knew for certain the context of the email, which left him in a holding pattern. If what she said was true—that she'd turned over an email with the evidence—then she had nothing to worry about. If what she said was a lie, and she'd been working with Quetech all along to launder the money, she'd face the consequences of her actions. The outcome was out of his hands. Either way, they were stuck together for the next three days.

An eternity considering his conflicted feelings for her. Without any evidence, he was flying solo. The attack in the garage had only gotten him so much leeway on handling the witness. He'd called in a welfare check at his house, but the car was gone and the police hadn't noticed anything suspicious. Maybe Ruth was taking her neighborhood watch duties too seriously.

Beth slid open the pocket door, looking sleepy and delightfully tousled. Her hair cascaded down her back and her leaf-green eyes blinked in droopy confusion. She appeared petite and vulnerable in the dimly lit, narrow corridor. He thought of Timothy Swan and hesitated. She was his witness. His responsibility. This time was different, though. As long as she came through with the evidence, she'd have protection.

"What time is it?" she asked, stifling a yawn.

At least one of them had gotten some sleep. "Midnight. Grab your stuff. This is our stop."

Though he'd confiscated her phone, he'd kept a close watch on her for the past few hours. He stood a better chance of living to a ripe old age if he maintained a healthy suspicion. He hadn't given her an opportunity to contact anyone else.

She tossed him a grumpy scowl. "Be right out."

"I thought accountants were morning people."

"It's not the morning. It's the middle of the night."

The door slammed in his face, and he stifled a grin. There was something oddly intimate in seeing her without the usual polite filters in place.

True to her word, she reappeared moments later. She'd caught her hair in a ponytail and slung her backpack over one shoulder. He urged her ahead of him, his attention sharp.

They made their way down the narrow staircase and into the chill Minnesota evening. An enclosed walkway separated the train from the depot, and their footsteps echoed through the space. He surveyed the half-dozen passengers who emerged with them into the vaulted lobby but saw nothing out of the ordinary.

The train had arrived early, making up time for the earlier delay. To his surprise, there appeared to be an FBI agent lounging against the ticket counter, a half-read newspaper in his hand. Had the Feds changed their mind about the jurisdiction?

The agent studied his phone before checking the crowd. No doubt comparing them to a photograph. The man caught sight of Beth and pocketed the device. He was definitely here for her. Corbin's annoyance flared. Someone should have notified him. Had new information come to light?

The agent strode toward them.

Corbin resisted an eye roll. The field agent had the same nondescript look as most FBI agents. His hair and eyes were brown, his build average. His face was clean-shaven, and his cargo pants crisp. The academy must stamp them out in a factory. He'd even dressed in an identifying windbreaker. If he turned, he'd reveal large letters spelling FBI across the back of his jacket.

He was beefy but not exactly fit. One of those men who used to be able to spend an hour in the gym three times a week to maintain his fitness and hadn't realized he was aging out of the routine.

The agent approached them and flashed his

identification. "I'm Agent Smith. Are you Elizabeth Greenwood?"

She glanced between the two men. "I, uh, I am. Yes."

"I'm here to take you in for questioning. Come with me, ma'am."

Corbin's scalp tingled. Something didn't feel right. "I'll be going with her."

"You can call your boyfriend later," Agent Smith said to Beth. "You're in a lot of trouble, Miss Greenwood."

Corbin's pulse jumped.

Agent Smith didn't know Corbin's identity. If the Feds had been informed of Beth's arrival, they'd be aware there was an accompanying agent from Homeland Security.

This man was no FBI agent.

FOUR

"Wait, w-what?" Beth stuttered.

Corbin wrapped his arm around her waist and gave a squeeze. "She's not going anywhere without me."

The two men stared each other down, each taking the other's measure.

"Suit yourself," Agent Smith replied without breaking eye contact.

Corbin studied the agent's clothing. The cargo pants and boots were better suited to tactical gear than questioning an accountant. He took a closer look at the jacket. The sleeves were marked with the usual insignia, but the edge of the *B* curled upward on the left arm. His nerve endings vibrated. Government-issued jackets were made better. That jacket had been bought off the internet—a cut-rate costume knockoff.

Corbin broke eye contact and cataloged his surroundings. An elderly security guard dozed behind a kiosk near the front desk. No help there.

"I want a lawyer," Corbin demanded. "You can't do this."

"You can call a lawyer when we get to the office." The agent flipped back the edges of his jacket, revealing his holstered gun. "Don't make any trouble. It won't go well for you."

"All right. But at least tell me what this is all about."

"Ask your girlfriend. Now start walking."

The man didn't see him as a threat, or he'd have refused Corbin's request outright. An advantage, given the circumstances.

Corbin leaned away from Beth. "What's this all about, *honey*?"

Her bewilderment was genuine, a fact he'd use in their favor.

"It's, u-uh…" she stuttered. "It's probably just something to do with work."

"I hope they're paying you overtime." He chuckled. Hoping she'd forgive him later, he planted a kiss on her temple and whispered, "Ask to use the restroom."

Beth pivoted on her heel and raised her voice, "I need to stop in the restroom."

The impostor agent shook his head. "We're behind schedule already."

Corbin shrugged. "Then another delay won't matter."

"I won't take long." Beth danced from foot to foot. "I'll hurry."

"Don't be a jerk, man," Corbin volunteered before the man could speak.

"Fine."

As they crossed the lobby, Corbin tucked her against his side and nuzzled the top of her head. "Look up. There are cameras. Make sure they get a good view of us."

If something went south, at least there'd be evidence they'd arrived at the station.

The fraudulent agent trailed behind them. The man pulled his phone from his pocket and typed.

Using the distraction, Corbin sped up their pace. "When we turn the corner, don't go into the restroom. Keep walking straight out the front door, and don't look back."

She turned her wide, frightened gaze on him. "What's going on? Why does he think you're my boyfriend?"

A bleary-eyed, uniformed train employee holding a phone to his ear strode toward them, a cup of coffee in his opposite hand. Corbin nudged his arm. The cup teetered, and hot liquid spilled over the edge. The employee yelped and dropped his cup.

Corbin muttered an apology.

He spun Beth toward him, cupping her face. "I don't care what the back of his jacket says, that's not an FBI agent."

He glanced behind him. The fraudulent agent

skidded through the puddle and went down hard on his hip. Muttering a string of curses directed at the employee, he pushed upright.

"Where should I go?" Beth asked, keeping her gaze fixed forward. "How will we find each other again?"

"I'll meet you," Corbin said, recalling the last time he'd visited the city. "There's a bar called Alary's on Seventh Street between Jackson and Robert. It's about six blocks north and west of here." No other businesses would be open at midnight. "If I'm not there in twenty minutes, call the police and tell them everything you know."

He slipped her phone into the trash. A memory from the parking garage flashed in his head. The navy coat, the dark ball cap, the flash of yellow. Not a Bears cap. The yellowing lettering spelled FBI. Fake agents. And they'd followed them. Why hadn't they snatched her in Chicago when she set out on foot? Why wait until now?

Corbin retraced their steps. Even the small amount of residual pepper spray in his car had been distracting, and Beth had saturated at least one of the two assailants' clothing. No one could drive very far in that condition, let alone stroll through the crowd at the station. He'd have to clean up first. Maybe the second man had stayed behind, he wasn't visible here. The delay had allowed Beth to safely board the train. The pepper spray had saved her twice.

"Are you sure I should just leave?" she whispered harshly. "What about you?"

She seemed genuinely concerned, and he studied her face. For now, he'd assume she wasn't lying. She knew well enough the men she'd tangled with earlier were dangerous.

"I'll be fine," he said. "I'm sorry about having to pretend back there."

He urged her to walk faster. Depending on how the next few minutes played out, he might not get another chance to apologize.

"That's all right. I know what you're trying to do."

"We'll get through this." He gave her arm an encouraging squeeze. "Go."

They rounded the corner, and she darted for the exit.

Corbin pressed open the restroom door and stepped back. The fraudulent agent caught up with him as the door swung shut once more. Corbin eyed the exit and assessed the few sleepy civilians populating the lobby.

"That must have hurt." Corbin indicated the dark splotch on the man's cargo pants. "You went down hard back there."

"Shut it."

"No need to be rude."

Corbin checked the enormous restored antique clock at the far end of the vaulted lobby. The minutes ticked by, and the fraudulent agent rocked back on his heels. Beth was gaining a good head start.

"What's taking her so long?" Agent Smith muttered.

"Women," Corbin replied with a shrug. After making a point of scrolling through the emails on his phone, he pounded on the door. "Hey honey, everything all right in there?"

The impostor muttered an oath. "Go in and get her."

"I can't go in there," Corbin dodged.

"She's your girlfriend. Get her."

Corbin pushed open the door and counted to ten before returning.

The blow caught him beneath the chin. Stars flared at the edges of his vision and pain exploded through his jaw. He rotated with the punch, making it appear as though he was more stunned than what the jolt had delivered. Bracing one shoulder against the wall, he slid to the floor. His face averted, he angled his foot for traction, one arm flexed.

"You helped her escape, didn't you?" The imposter reached into his jacket. "You shouldn't have done that."

Corbin assessed his options and made a quick decision. "I don't know what you're talking about."

He dove, twisting his body. Using his weight, he slammed into the man. Caught off balance, the two flew backward. Corbin held tight, following the man to the tile floor, his elbow digging into his opponent's solar plexus. Winded from the blow, the man gasped for breath. Corbin yanked the impostor's gun from the holster and staggered upright.

The man pressed his hand against his chest and rolled to his side. "You're tougher than you look, super boy."

Tucking the gun against his side, Corbin bent and reached for his glasses. *Super boy?* Another reference to mild-mannered reporter, Clark. He really needed to invest in a new pair of frames.

"On your feet." Corbin gestured with the man's gun. "Let's take this outside."

He had control of the situation, but he wasn't taking any chances. He needed the man away from civilians and potential hostages.

"Get out of this while you still can," the man said, lurching upright. "Your girlfriend is going to get you killed."

"Not your concern."

"What are you? An army boy? I recognize that blow to the solar plexus. It's dirty, but it gets the job done."

"My turn for questions," Corbin said. "Who do you work for?"

"Ask your girlfriend," the man sneered. "You have no idea what she's gotten you into, do you?"

"Then tell me."

The man chuckled. "Let me go and I'll think about letting you live. I'm former military myself. It's tough becoming a civilian, isn't it? They oughta ween us off adrenaline like we're junkies, but they don't. They turn us into killers and then dump us stateside to mow the lawn and take out the trash like every other chump. It's never enough."

That first year behind a desk, Corbin had thought he was going mad. He'd jog the stairs to release the extra energy. Being assigned more fieldwork had taken the edge off. His superiors had been weaning him off the adrenaline.

"Enough talk," Corbin replied, his voice gruff.

"Look, super boy, no woman is worth dying for. Come work for me. I'm always looking for a good man."

"Not interested."

Corbin grasped a handful of the man's windbreaker and shoved him forward. He kept the gun pressed tightly against the man's side, out of view.

After patting the guy down for additional weapons, Corbin did a quick search of the man's pockets but only discovered the fraudulent credentials.

A decent counterfeit but the identification didn't stand up to closer inspection. The man's first name was listed as Van, his surname as Smith. There was a good chance Van was his real name. Corbin stuffed the folded leather case into his pocket for future investigation. Discovering the source of the forgery might lead to more information.

The commotion was catching the attention of the few people milling around the train station. As they passed an older couple, the middle-aged woman clutched her purse and cringed.

"Sorry, ma'am," Corbin said with a smile. "Just getting some fresh air."

She met his reassuring grin with puzzled confusion. He pushed through the exit doors and searched his surroundings. The platform was deserted. With his free hand, he reached into his pocket for his phone.

The impostor glanced over his shoulder. "What are you going to do, super boy? Call the police? Your girlfriend is a thief. You'll both go to jail."

A bullet ripped Corbin's upper arm an instant before he heard the report. Pain seared through his shoulder. His knees gave out, and he collapsed. His gun careened across the pavement.

The impostor stalked toward the discarded weapon. Light-headed, Corbin reached into his jacket for his Glock. The man stomped painfully on his shoulder, paralyzing his arm.

Corbin hissed. "Does this mean you're taking back the job offer?"

"You didn't think I was working alone, did you?" The man guffawed. "You should have run while you had a chance, but you had to be a superhero. I'll ask you one more time, where's your girlfriend?"

Corbin's gut twisted. He should have told Beth to call the police immediately instead of waiting for him. "She's long gone, Van."

The imposter's eyes flickered before he caught himself.

"Your accountant won't get very far."

"Far enough."

"Raynor!" Van called to someone out of Corbin's sightline. "Get the car. Check the streets north of here. She'll go toward the city." He shook his head. "What are we going to do with you?"

Pain radiated from Corbin's arm, and his stomach roiled. He had to buy Beth more time. "How did you track us, Van?"

"Who says we tracked you? Maybe your girlfriend set you up. Maybe this is all happening just the way it's supposed to."

"You're lying. She nearly cleaned your clock in that garage."

Van gave a hallow chuckle. "You're making a lot of trouble for me, super boy. You oughta know that Raynor wants revenge for the pepper spray."

He applied more pressure to Corbin's shoulder. "Guess that's a start."

As the impostor crouched for his weapon, Corbin lunged. His fingertips closed around the muzzle, but Van got hold of the handle. The mercenary had the leverage, a miscalculation on Corbin's part, and he jerked the gun free. Corbin dove sideways, bracing for the shot. If he moved fast enough, maybe the bullet would miss hitting anything vital. Blood rushed in his ears. Two tours of Afghanistan and he was going to die stateside at a train station.

Van's eyes widened. Arms akimbo, he twitched once, then twice, and tumbled forward. Beth stood behind him, a smashed umbrella with a wooden handle dangling from her clenched hands.

"Not so tough without your gun," she declared.

A bullet shattered the pillar beside Beth, spraying bits of concrete. She shrieked and threw her arms before her face.

"Get down!" Corbin hollered.

Dizzy with adrenaline, she immediately cowered behind the sheltering pillar.

The mercenary groaned and stirred. Dragging a hand over the back of his head, he pitched to his knees. The umbrella hadn't been as sturdy as she'd hoped. He was stunned, but he'd soon recover. Corbin hesitated only a moment before leaping over the man. Beth frantically searched their surroundings. No security guards were running out of the building, no sirens sounded in the distance. No help was coming anytime soon.

"There are two." Corbin grasped Van's gun, pocketing the extra weapon. "We have to get out of here. Quick."

"Shouldn't we call the police?"

The street was deserted this time of night. No passing cars to call in the disturbance. The building was old and solid. Maybe the sound hadn't carried inside.

"No time," Corbin said. "We'll be dead before they get here."

Another bullet ricocheted off the pavement, shattering a divot in the concrete. The spray of gravel peppered her legs.

Beth squeezed tighter to the pillar. Corbin had a point about the time. "I thought the second guy was bringing the car around," she called.

They were trapped about ten feet apart. If one of them crossed the distance, they'd be a target.

"Guess not," Corbin called back.

They had at least one advantage. The shooter was aiming at them through a maze of pillars. Corbin kept his weapon arm extended, then dropped the gun to his side. She watched as he calculated his next move. There were too many unknowns in the vicinity to return fire, and they were dealing with a shooter unconcerned with collateral damage.

Though trying to view the unfolding events with a critical eye, she was still fighting against the shell shock. Crouched by the pillar, she held her palms pressed against her temples, her eyes brimming. Keeping low, Corbin dashed for her.

He snatched her ice-cold hand and urged her upright. "Stay with me. I'll let you break down later, all right?"

"I'm fine." She glared at him, her eyes clearing. "Just startled, that's all."

Think about the details. That's what her dad would say. She played the confrontation in the parking garage through her head like a movie reel.

Details. The assailant had been dressed in black. Cargo pants. Boots. Tactical gear. She hadn't gotten a good look at the driver. Two men. A ball cap with lettering. The same men. They'd been tracked from Chicago. How?

"You up for a run?" Corbin asked.

"Lead the way," she replied immediately, only a slight wobble in her voice.

She wouldn't break down. Not now. Not in front of him. Later though, when she was alone, she feared the events of the evening were bound to catch up with her.

Corbin tugged into her into a quick embrace. She didn't resist. Despite her best intentions, her whole body trembled violently. She sensed he was trying to infuse her with his strength for the coming ordeal. She sagged briefly, then she squeezed his hand and nodded. No more hesitating.

He peered around the corner and quickly ducked back. She did the same on her side. Neither of the men was anywhere in sight.

No bullets responded to their furtive movements.

Taking a deep breath, he said, "Let me know if you can't keep up."

She was determined to remain analytical, above the emotion. She'd push everything aside and deal with the feelings later. As long as they kept moving, they had a chance.

"You, too," she said with a challenging glare.

That was good. Her voice had been strong. She wasn't dead weight. Forcing air into her lungs, she concentrated on her surroundings. Breath. Focus. She was growing accustomed to the heightened level of stress.

Together they raced toward the street, and she surveyed the scene through her dad's eyes. That's how Corbin would be reacting. There wasn't much traffic, which was both an advantage and a disadvantage. The deserted streets limited civilian encounters but lacked feasible opportunities for cover.

He glanced up at the street sign and cut north.

"Do you know where you're going?" she asked.

He'd given her pretty specific directions earlier.

"I worked a case in Minneapolis, St. Paul. I have some knowledge of the area."

The night was cold, but she didn't feel the chill or the wind. Her coat was inadequate for the conditions, but as long as they were running, she'd be fine.

A garbage truck drove by, and they used the bulk and noise to cover their path to the next corner. The truck flashed its turn signal, and they raced down the street in the opposite direction.

Her heart hammering, she glanced around. "Where are they?"

"I'm guessing they circled back to retrieve their car," Corbin said. "Wheels have the advantage. Which means we'll need to get some distance in the next few minutes."

"*Who* are they?" Beth tightened her grip on his hand. "How did they find us?"

"It's the same two from the parking garage." Dodging left, he turned down an alley and urged them into the shadows. "The guy you bludgeoned just now, I think his first name is Van. The surname listed on his identity, Smith, is a little too convenient. Probably a cover. They were posing as FBI agents earlier this evening. I'm guessing they planned on picking you up at Quetech. When they caught you alone in the garage, they took the opportunity."

Corbin whipped off his coat before hastily wrapping the material around his arm.

Her chest seized. He was bleeding. In all the commotion, she'd forgotten the initial shot. She'd been crouching behind the shelter of a pillar. Waiting.

She stared in mute horror at the traces of his blood dripping from his fingertips.

"You're hurt!" She gasped.

"It's nothing."

Headlights trolled past the opposite end of the alley.

He pressed Beth behind a dumpster overflowing with rancid fruit, out of sight. "Sorry for the smell."

"I choose life." She held her hoodie sleeve over her nose. "I'll worry about the smell later."

Keeping a hair's breadth between them, he blocked her from the lights and the worst of the wind. Everything else faded into the background. The weather. The temperature. Only the strong feel of his muscles beneath her fingertips remained. She shoved her fear aside and concentrated on the next few minutes. They were on foot. They were in the open. They were vulnerable. Attack each problem in turn.

"Follow Me. Close," he ordered gently.

Her shoes skidded over discarded kitchen scraps, half-frozen to the pavement. "Don't worry. I'm stuck to you like glue."

He had the gun and the training, after all. The next time he needed to audit his accountant, she'd return the favor. For now, she'd follow his lead. He was the expert.

"How far can you run?" he asked.

She could jog for miles, but a sustained sprint took more energy. "Full-out? About six blocks."

He took her hand once more. "Let's go."

They dashed between the two buildings, then crossed the street and disappeared beneath the trees of an area marked as Mears Park. He cut a diagonal toward the next street. A sign for Lowertown Foods glowed in the darkness. The late hour meant the building was virtually empty. He led her inside. The lights were jarring, and she blinked, adjusting to the glare.

"Keep your head down," Corbin whispered.

Her face angled, she clutched his arm in the role of infatuated girlfriend. Just a couple of people out for a midnight stroll. Nothing to see here, folks.

The cashier glanced up, but there was no security guard in sight. They wove their way through pallets of shrink-wrapped merchandise blocking the aisles. The double stock doors were propped open, and they slipped through unnoticed. Corbin led them out the back exit and into a courtyard.

The next block over was a well-lit, open parking lot with no cover. She focused on her breathing once more. They were easy targets in the open.

Corbin paused long enough to study her face. "Holding up?"

She'd have preferred to be in a hot bath while sipping a cup of tea and reading a novel. She kept that information to herself. Once they stopped moving, they were a bull's-eye.

"I'm fine," she said, her voice only slightly breathless. She adjusted the straps of her backpack. "Don't worry about me. Get us out of here."

Her breath puffed vapor into the chill night air. She was frightened but determined, and she refused to be the weak link between them. They weren't getting caught because she couldn't keep up.

He led them across the next street and beneath the awning of an office building. A truck whizzed past, and they ducked into the receded entry. Her heart hammered against her ribs. The driver was older. The glow of a streetlight shimmered off the windshield. A gray-haired man hunched over the steering wheel. Not their pursuers.

The stoplight at the end of the block halted traffic, but the row of cars had a clear sight line of any movement. She caluclated the odds the two men were in the line of cars. Her pulse jumped. The odds were excellent.

She tugged on Corbin's sleeve. "We need cover."

"Or a distraction."

He yanked on the chrome door handle, and a high-pitched alarm screamed into the night. Corbin winced.

Her hands hovering over her ears, Beth cringed. "Why did you do that?"

"Like I said. Distraction. Let's go."

They skirted around the building while remaining hidden in the shadows. Even with the alarm blaring in the background, Corbin's harsh breathing sounded loud beside her. She was reaching the end of her endurance, but she wasn't about to admit as much. She'd find the reserves of strength somewhere.

Corbin pointed. "There."

A painted sign read Alary's. The pub was in the middle of a line of attached nondescript turn-of-the-century buildings. Front and back exits. No access from the sides. Sirens sounded in the distance. Corbin's plan was working.

"Just to be safe," he said, "let's circle around to the back of the building."

"Okay."

The one-way alley was wide enough for a single garbage truck to pass through and dimly lit. The restaurant had a dumpster out back. Something scuttled across the concrete, and Beth cringed.

Holding an index finger to his lips, Corbin signaled for silence. The sirens grew closer. For the next few minutes, the police would be checking the building with the triggered security alarm. They'd have their flashlights drawn, gloved hands tented against the tinted glass for a better look inside. They'd see the door was locked and call in a false alarm. She figured they had about twenty more minutes before the cruisers abandoned the search.

How well did the two men chasing them know the city? Hopefully, not well. It wouldn't take a genius to figure out that a bar was the only place open this time of night. Thankfully, Alary's didn't believe in neon signs. A neighborhood joint by the looks of the building, the bar and grill didn't stand out unless the patrons knew where to look.

She held her breath, but no cars appeared at the end of the street.

Think like a cop.

A sliver of light showed where the kitchen door was propped open, venting heat from the stoves into the brisk autumn evening. Corbin smoothed his hair and uncurled his jacket from his arm, then draped the material over his shoulder to cover the blood.

Beth remained frozen. Her hands wrapped around her body, her lips tight to control the trembling. She was fine. Nothing wrong here. No reason to fall apart. The second kidnapping attempt in so many hours. Just another day.

Clearing his throat, Corbin said, "We're looking a little battered. You might want to, um—" he gestured ineffectively "—the less attention we draw to ourselves the better."

"I don't know what I look like." She rammed her hands into the pockets of her hoodie, stretching the material to mid-thigh. "What do I need?"

As he hesitated, she took in his face in darting glances that ricocheted off the alley and the back door of the restaurant.

He gently straightened the collar of her hoodie and smoothed the straps of her backpack. Using his awkward left hand, he stroked the blond hair from her forehead then tucked a stray lock behind the curve of her ear. She shivered in response, hoping he mistook her reaction for the chill in the air.

She remained still and silent beneath his ministrations, her breathing slowing, but still irregular. Her eyes were watchful. One mistake. One flash of headlights falling on them, and they were finished.

He cleared his throat again. "Just follow me and pretend everything is perfectly normal."

FIVE

Corbin's arm throbbed. The least of his worries. Beth was afraid the authorities couldn't protect her. What if she was right?

He'd been searching for the truth since the day someone had set Timothy Swan's file on his desk, and he'd unleashed a sleeping giant. There was no telling what was going to happen next, or how long it was going to take to unravel this mess.

Beth's eyes remained watchful. Her alabaster skin glowed in the halo of the streetlights. There was no time for words of comfort. No time to tell her everything was going to be all right.

She was gazing at him in question, her expression trusting.

The realization hit him in the gut, knocking the breath from his lungs.

He'd been holding her at arm's length, keeping his distance. Not Beth. She'd put her trust in him. She'd put her faith in him to keep her safe without even knowing if he was up to the task. He was flying alone, without backup.

They were on their own until they had proof of the evidence. They could call police, but that unleased a jurisdictional nightmare. She had a false identity. She had no proof she'd sent an email that effectively exonerated her. Better to call in something anonymously. Except that left them vulnerable.

There was another choice.

Could he hand her over to the FBI and walk away? They didn't trust her. Corbin did. Timothy Swan's death still weighed heavy on his soul. They hadn't taken the threat seriously enough.

For better or worse, Beth trusted him to see this through.

In the distance, sirens blared. Too far away. Not the cruisers checking the building alarm. Had someone finally alerted the police to the commotion at the train station? What would they discover?

He chafed her upper arms. "Let's go inside, sit down, and regroup."

"Okay."

The warmth from the kitchen hit them like a humid wall scented with stale frying grease. There were two cooks in the galley-style room, their backs to the center, their attention focused on the equipment.

Corbin strode down the middle, Beth in tow.

A robust cook in a greasy apron turned. "Hey!" His flailing spatula sent a splatter of oil arcing through the air. "You can't be in here."

Corbin offered a friendly smile. "Sorry. Got turned around in the alley. We'll get out of your way."

He led Beth through the swinging door into the back of the bar, then ushered them to a tall-backed booth. The air smelled of beer and stale French fries, and the tabletop was sticky. He reluctantly released his hold.

She glanced down. "I'll be right back. I need to wash my hands."

Her gaze skipped away. She needed to wash off the blood.

His blood.

"Okay."

As he slid into the seat, he surveyed their surroundings. Near closing time, most of the patrons had already gone home, leaving the bar sparsely occupied. The layout was shotgun style, and he chose his vantage point for an optimal view of both the front and back exits. They had enough cover to go unnoticed, but he'd still be able to see if the men chasing them entered the building. He concentrated on measuring his breathing, letting his heartbeat slow to a normal rhythm.

Beth returned a short time later, her eyes drawn

and red-rimmed. She was exhausted. She rarely stayed up past the evening news. He'd heard her admitting as much when a coworker asked her about a late-night talk show.

"Are you all right?" She stared at her hands. "You need medical attention."

"The bullet only grazed me. It's already stopped bleeding."

The pain was radiating down his shoulder, but he kept that tidbit of information to himself. She'd been through enough tonight. She needed to know that everything was going to be all right. She needed to know he had control of the situation.

"We shouldn't stay here," her voice was low and urgent. "What if they find us?"

"They're not going to stick around with the police patrolling the area. We need to pass some time. Maybe ten minutes. Just until the police realize they have a false alarm."

He'd tossed her phone. The most likely source of the tracking. He should have taken Ruth's phone call more seriously. He should have dumped the phone earlier.

"How *did* they find us?" she asked. "I still don't know how you discovered I was taking the train. Maybe they followed us the same way."

"I can safely say they didn't use the same method." He sagged back against the torn Naugahyde booth. "I saw your ticket when you tripped over the trash bin."

His confession earned a weak smile. "You said it was your keen powers of intellect and deduction."

"They must have traced your phone. That's the only explanation."

Snatches of conversation whirled like a kaleidoscope through his head. *Maybe this is all happening the way it's supposed to. Maybe your girlfriend set you up.*

Despite the impostor's attempt to sway him, Beth's involvement didn't fit. "Where'd you get the umbrella?"

"From a stand by the guard station." She heaved a ragged sigh. "I thought it might make a good weapon in a pinch."

"Clever."

She'd saved his hide, yet he couldn't trust her. Not completely. Not yet. There was too much at stake. Too bad life wasn't like detective novels. There was never any sure way to tell if someone was lying or not.

She glanced at his wrapped arm. "Didn't save you from taking a bullet. We need to get you to a hospital. You're risking an infection or something."

"It's nothing."

"Let me see. I'll be the judge."

Her voice was stronger, reminding him of everything he admired about her. She was bright, self-confident and tough. He'd let her issue the orders—for now. He knew what it was like to feel as though life was spinning out of control. He knew what it was like to crave a sense of control over something—anything—when the world was crumbling.

Leaning in, she stretched over the table. He caught a hint of her floral scent, a welcome respite to the overpowering odor of stale, spilled beer. Her fingers explored the edges of his torn coat, their touch feather-light. Her normally sleek hair was slightly mussed. This close, he noted the strands were actually several different shades of blond that blended together to form the golden color, the roots slightly darker.

A weak lightbulb cast shadows from a dusty, overhead lamp advertising a classic brand of beer with a bucolic campsite near a waterfall. There was something familiar about the light, and he concentrated on the scene, forcing his attention away from the graceful sweep of her neck.

His dad had a clock advertising the same beer in the garage. The background scrolled by, an optical illusion, making the water appear to ripple. He and his brother had broken the clock face while playing four square in the garage when it was too cold to play outside. The accident had cost them a month of Saturday morning cartoons.

The memory seemed both very near, and a lifetime away.

His phone rang, and Beth startled upright. Their faces were inches apart, her arms braced on the tabletop. His attention dropped to her lips. Butterflies took flight in his stomach. The phone rang again, and she sat back in her seat. Oddly breathless, he didn't trust his voice to reply until the phone had rung three times.

His arm throbbed.

Concentrating on the pain, he tightened the makeshift bandage before answering with a curt, "Yeah."

"Your accountant is blowing up the wires," his team leader, Baker, stated without preamble.

"How'd they find out about her?" Corbin asked.

His relationship with his superior had been rocky in the beginning. Corbin's transition from working in the field to working in an office had been about as smooth as a dirt road in Kabul. Life and death had turned into paperwork and bureaucratic pandering. *They ought to treat us like junkies—adrenaline junkies.* He'd been warned about what to expect by others. They'd gone over everything in his debriefing. Words on paper were weak in comparison to reality. Returning to civilian life had been a shock.

In an odd twist, Timothy Swann's death had changed the dynamic for the better. They'd put new protocols in place. New levels of trust were established. Over the past two years, Baker had given him more field assignments. The change of pace and scenery had alleviated his restless energy. Everyone got along just fine now.

"This isn't about the money laundering." Baker paused. "The chief financial officer at Quetech Industries, Sam Cross, was shot at point-blank range sometime between noon and four yesterday The official narrative is that he stopped home for lunch and walked in on a burglary. The wife found him when she got off work."

Corbin pictured Baker restlessly pacing his living room. He had the high, prominent forehead and bulging nose of a gumshoe from a forties era black-and-white movie, along with the rumpled appearance to match. In another life, he might have been wasted, but despite his unlikely appearance, he was a genius at tracing thousands of tangled cyber threads.

"You're not buying the burglary story?" Corbin asked.

"Nothing was taken. The place was tossed, but the wife says nothing is missing. The alarm didn't go off, and the wife claims Cross never forgot to set it. Doesn't sound like the work of a suburban housebreaker."

"What about the rest?"

Beth's gaze was sharp and watchful. He didn't want to frighten her until he knew exactly what was happening.

"The police would like to question Beth about his death and her involvement in an embezzlement scheme. The victim, Cross, conveniently left some notes on his desk to that effect."

"Notes on the work desk." Corbin guffawed. "Imagine that."

"My thoughts exactly."

Corbin glanced at Beth's ashen face, and a knot formed in his stomach. "What now?"

"I guess that depends on if she had anything to do with his murder."

"Not unless she has a doppelganger. I've been with her all night. I don't see her taking down Cross alone."

Beth was looking edgy. She knew they were talking about her. He wasn't exactly speaking in code. Corbin kept his expression neutral, relaxed. No need to worry. Everything was going to be all right. Just making a plan of attack for the next few hours.

Baker grunted. "The police are smart enough to know that, too. They just want to scare her. Apply a little leverage and see if she blabs about the embezzlement."

"Nice."

He'd used the tactic before, but it didn't sit well this time around.

"Either way, stay off the radar," Baker said. "They're shaking the bushes, seeing what darts out of the shadows. If she's got the evidence like you say, this is the bad guys trying to smoke her out. Don't let them." The tapping of keys sounded in the background. "It's too dangerous. The FBI is still shrugging off jurisdiction. Mark my words, if she comes through with the accounting trace, they'll be knocking down our door. Always like to let everyone else do the legwork and then swoop in with the arrests."

"There's more." Corbin chose his next words carefully. "We had a welcoming committee at the station. The same guys from Chicago."

"They got wings?"

Corbin considered the time line. "Takes hours to drive from Minneapolis if you're motivated. Took us a little longer by train. I think they killed Cross, then came for Beth."

"Busy day for those two," Baker grumbled. "You sure they don't have wings?"

Baker might question the time line, but it wasn't impossible. Until Corbin learned otherwise, the window was large enough for a murder and a road trip.

Either the chief financial officer was involved in the scheme, or he'd discovered the money laundering. "Whether or not they had anything to do with Cross, they were here tonight."

"Okay. I'll see if the coroner has pinned down a time of death." Another lengthy pause was accompanied by the sound of papers shuffling. "I'm willing to believe your accountant has something of value considering the past twenty-four hours. You think you're still being tailed?"

"I doubt it. I dumped the electronics."

"Good. I'll buy you some time on our end. If you turn her over to the Feds, it's out of my hands. But it's your call. You do what you think is best."

They'd arrest her for the possession of false identification, but she'd be in custody. There was no greater protection. "Is it safer?"

"The FBI office said something about a wire-tap and bait."

Not safer. "Let's keep this between you and me for the next few days."

"Agreed. Where are you now?"

"Minneapolis. The St. Paul area." Corbin weighed his options. "We'll turn it around."

"Chicago is too hot. Can you make it back to headquarters?"

"Public transportation is going to be risky. I don't want anything with our name on it."

Which ruled out most modes of travel.

"Get some wheels," Baker said. "Should be something cheap for sale in that town."

"How's the department going to feel about the expense report?"

"This morning I authorized two last-minute plane tickets to Brussels. Cost me six thousand dollars. Try and do better than that."

"Will do," Corbin said.

"You sure you don't need backup? I can put pressure on the Feds."

Considering their recent encounter, the fewer people who knew about their whereabouts, the better. Corbin also didn't like the words "wire-tap" and "bait."

He'd made a tactical error by not ditching her phone earlier. He'd been holding out, waiting to see if someone made contact. He wouldn't make the same mistake again.

The less Beth was exposed, the better. "Too risky."

"Don't rule out the accountant. There's always the possibility she framed Cross to save her own hide. Watch your back with *Beth*."

The emphasis hit its mark.

Leave it to Baker to catch his slip. "Understood. Check the security footage from the train station in St. Paul. There's plenty of video of at least one of the men. Might turn up something."

"Will do," Baker said. "Don't get dead on me."

"Don't plan on it. This phone number won't be viable after today."

"Understood. Keep in contact."

Corbin hung up the phone and pressed his hand against the wound on his arm. The bleeding had stopped, but it wouldn't take much to start it up again. He was holding his arm gingerly, trying to minimize his movements. He wasn't risking medical attention. Hospitals were required by law to notify law enforcement of bullet wounds.

There was another advantage. No medical reports to file, either. Baker might have responded differently had he known of Corbin's injury.

"Were you talking about Sam?" Beth reached across the table and touched his wrist. "What is it? What's wrong?"

Despite Baker's conjecture, he doubted Beth had been involved in Sam Cross's death. The men from the parking garage were the most likely suspects. If Beth had uncovered the money laundering, there was no reason to believe Sam hadn't done the same. Or there was the possibility Sam had been involved, and his services were no longer required.

"You're under investigation for embezzlement," he said grimly, retracting his hand. There was no use beating around the bush. This next bit of information was bound to test her fortitude, but she deserved to know what was happening. "They also want to question you about something else."

"What could be worse than embezzling?"

"Murder."

* * *

Beth felt as though all the oxygen had been sucked out of the room. "Murder?"

She went cold, gripped by an icy paralysis. While she suspected the thugs from Cayman Holdings, Limited were on the wrong side of the law, until now, her part in this business had been on the white-collar-crime side of events. If anything, she thought they'd try and frame her for the money laundering; she never considered they'd frame her for murder.

"Who?" Her hands and lips had gone numb, and she struggled to form words. "Who do they think I've murdered?"

"They don't think you murdered him. They just want you for questioning. Sam Cross."

"The chief financial officer?" She rested her head in the circle of her arms. "We were just joking about all the graphs in his PowerPoint."

Only moments before she'd been feeling sorry for herself. She'd spent the past few hours retracing all the steps that had led her to this place. She'd thought of all the ways things might have turned out differently. She'd second-guessed every decision she'd made since deciding to become an accountant. All of that paled in comparison to the news of Sam's death.

Her life was in danger, but she was alive. "He wasn't involved. Why would they kill him?"

"We won't know anything for certain until we comb through his financial records."

"I already did that." Her focus sharpened. "You can't honestly believe he had anything to do with the money laundering?"

While Sam had the means and opportunity, he lacked a motive. She'd scoured his transactions and discovered nothing out of the ordinary.

Corbin's brow furrowed. "We can't rule out anyone at this stage. Someone is slamming the door on this business by eliminating anyone with knowledge of the transactions. Who brought you in to do the audit?"

"Matt Shazier, the CEO."

"Not Cross."

"Nope." She shook her head, as though warding off the grim news. "I don't believe Sam was involved. He filed his receipts by date. There's a picture on his desk that was taken several years ago, and he's wearing the same tie he wore yesterday. That is not the sort of man who launders money for terrorists." Stars swam at the corners of her vision. "He had a son going to UCLA. Sam was so proud of him."

In the picture, Sam was holding his son's hand while the boy clutched the ribbon end of a balloon. He'd never risk becoming involved in something that jeopardized his family.

"College isn't cheap," Corbin said, more to himself than to her.

"That's why people work overtime and take out loans. They don't get involved with a terrorist." No matter what Corbin thought, she didn't believe Sam had anything to do with anything illegal. Another horror occurred to her. "What happened? How did he die?"

Her stomach churned. The terror from the parking garage was fresh. She couldn't bear the thought of him suffering.

"He was shot late yesterday afternoon." Corbin studied her face. "Close range. His death was instant. He probably never even saw what was coming."

"Wait, what…?" The news had fragmented her thoughts into a thousand tiny shards. "He was killed late yesterday afternoon? Why do they suspect me? I've been with you the whole time."

Corbin quirked an eyebrow. "I'm aware of that."

A waitress appeared at the end of their table, her dirty blond hair caught in a ponytail.

Attempting to maintain an air of calm indifference, Beth ordered a soda and declined anything to eat. The waitress tapped her pencil against her pad and glanced between them. She appeared to suspect something wasn't quite right about the new diners, but she wasn't commenting.

When she left, Beth said, "I have to go back. I have to clear my name."

Her stomach pitched. She was a cop's daughter. She knew how this worked. She'd be arrested for purchasing the false identification. At the very least, they'd drag her name through the newspapers. Her professional life was over. No one wanted an untrustworthy accountant on the payroll. Especially a forensic accountant with a rumored history of fraud.

"We'll clear your name later," Corbin said. "It's too dangerous to go back now."

"But—"

"The police are putting the pressure on you."

Beth groaned. "It's working."

"They want to see if you've got anything to do with an embezzling scheme."

"Embezzling?" She suddenly grew light-headed. "There's no embezzling. That's ridiculous. This is about money laundering, not theft."

"I think these guys have someone on the inside." Wouldn't take much to grease a few palms and weight the narrative toward Beth's guilt. "Embezzling is easier to sell in the press."

"The press?" she repeated, her voice weak.

Her plan had been deceptively simple and clear. Deliver the evidence and remain out of sight until the indictments made the news. The more steps she put between the evidence and the source of

information, the safer she was. She hadn't anticipated a false murder charge along with an accu-
sation of embezzling.

Corbin tightened the bandage on his arm, and
she caught herself. His face had taken on a waxy
appearance. He'd been wounded. His coat was
too dark to discern the amount of bleeding, but
this wasn't the time to sit around and feel sorry
for herself.

She'd have to trust that God had a plan for her
in all this.

Focusing on his injury and their next step took
her mind off the problems awaiting her down the
road. "We need to bandage your arm and get some
rest." The adrenaline was wearing off, and her
eyelids drooped. "We can't sit here forever. Where
do you suggest we go next?"

She was out of her league. While she'd rather
handle the situation independently, Corbin was
currently the expert on covert ops.

The kitchen door swung open, and Corbin
whipped around. Her heartbeat jerked. One of the
cooks they'd seen earlier appeared, an enormous
tray of nachos balanced on his outstretched hand.

Corbin's shoulders visibly relaxed. "Both at-
tacks took place in sparsely populated locations.
Tweedledum and Tweedledumber aren't taking
big risks. I think we lost them, but I don't know
for certain. I'm not taking any chances. We find

a crowded, well-lit hotel and spend the night. We can reassess in the morning."

"Reassess? What exactly does that mean?"

"We dump everything now and start over tomorrow. Phones, clothing. Everything. They were tracking us, and we need to make certain we've lost them. I'm guessing they got to your phone at work, but we start over. Just in case."

Fatigue and stress were making her cranky. "How exactly do we make sure we've lost them?"

"We'll find someplace that's crowded with a lot of security, and make sure we don't have a tail. Once we're squared away, we can travel. For now, we make sure we're not isolated."

"Okay, okay. We find a crowded hotel for tonight, and a crowded place to see if we're still being followed tomorrow. What about the Mall of America?"

"Too many places to hide. Too many exits. We need crowds. But we need them spread out. Like a sporting event."

The waitress set down their drinks. Beth reached for enough money to cover the bill, and then she added a generous tip. The waitress perked at the sight.

Beth assumed her most engaging smile. When seeking information, it was always best to flatter a local. Another tidbit of her dad's wisdom. "We're visiting from out of town, and we don't know much about the area. Your city is absolutely charming this time of year. Are there any events around town that might be interesting? Sporting events or something like that?"

The waitress wrapped one finger around the wispy end of her ponytail. "There's a hockey game at the arena tomorrow night. The Rangers are playing. I'm going this morning to get some autographs. There's also a harvest festival just north of town. It's quite an event. There's a corn maze and everything. My boyfriend and I are going next weekend."

"Thank you," Beth said. "That's exactly the sort of event I'm looking for. A harvest festival sounds like fun."

The waitress turned from the table before speaking over her shoulder, "Try the mini donuts. They're the best. But be careful in the corn maze. I got lost for an hour last year."

Beth flashed both thumbs. "Will do."

Corbin held his ice-filled cup to his bruised chin. "Nice work."

The timbre of his warm, deep voice sent a shiver of awareness through her.

Pulling up a map on his phone, he said, "I'm guessing the visiting hockey team will stay at the convention hotel." He clicked through a few more screens. "Looks like they have available rooms. I'll order an Uber."

"I got rid of my phone." Beth narrowed her gaze. "What about your phone?"

"Fine. If it makes you feel better, we'll ditch both our phones. We can pick up a couple of burners in the morning. Anything that might have been compromised has to be ditched."

"They can't have gotten to my bag. I left it at the train station."

"Would you rather be safe or dead? Nothing that's been out of your sight. The bag was out of your sight."

She huffed. "Fine."

She retrieved the zippered makeup pouch with her cash and fraudulent identification, along with the small, framed picture of her father. She hesitated only a moment before stuffing the picture in her pouch. On their way out, she dumped her backpack and extra clothing in the trash bin. The frugal part of her mourned the waste, but at least she'd traveled light.

There wasn't much to throw away.

"What now?" she asked.

Corbin's expression shifted.

As the waitress passed them in the opposite direction, he caught her attention. "My wife's ex-husband has been harassing us." He indicated the front of the building. "If anyone comes asking, you didn't see us, all right?"

The waitress cantilevered back, gazing toward

the front of the bar, then straightened and gave Corbin an admiring glance.

She turned toward Beth. "There's an exit through the kitchen that leads to the alley. You're better off with this fellow, sugar."

"Yep," Beth replied. He'd probably arrest her before this was all over, but right now, he was the only person in this mess who wasn't trying to kill her. "I sure am."

SIX

An hour later, the car delivered them to a downtown hotel near the convention center. Corbin had refused Beth's insistence that he visit a hospital or urgent care. Instead, they'd stopped at a drugstore along the way. Though his jaw was bruised and his arm bleeding, he wasn't injured otherwise. There was no need to make a fuss.

The most humiliating part of the evening had been letting Beth check them into the hotel room. Using her fraudulent identity, she'd booked them two adjoining rooms.

Corbin didn't bother hiding his scowl throughout the proceedings.

There was nothing in the Homeland Security handbook about letting the suspect in custody use an illegally obtained fraudulent identity to secure lodging, but he was fairly certain that sort of thing was frowned upon.

The hotel clerk flicked a glance between the two of them while his fingers tapped across the keyboard. Corbin softened his expression. No need to look like a menace. They'd call the police on them if he didn't get hold of himself.

The clerk was sharply dressed and thin with skin that mirrored the mahogany countertop and a high forehead above his sharp eyes. "Checkout time is at eleven. There's a complimentary breakfast served from six to nine."

Corbin glanced around the lobby. Knots of people laughed and talked, their chatter echoing off the high ceilings. "Is it always this busy?"

"Folks are in and out all night. Especially when the Rangers are in town. You're four floors up, though. You shouldn't be bothered by the noise."

Corbin was reasonably certain they'd lost the two men, but he was operating with an abundance of caution. "I'm sure we'll be fine."

"Thank you," Beth said, grasping the key cards.

Corbin exchanged a glance with Beth as they crossed the lobby. "If those two goons don't like crowds, we picked a good hotel."

"Mmm-hmm," she muttered noncommittally, stifling a yawn. As they stepped onto the elevator, she searched his face. "You look ill."

"I'm fine."

He'd already made enough mistakes. He refused to show vulnerability around her. She deserved to feel safe. He'd been viewing Beth as the perpetrator and not a target. He'd adjusted his thinking.

At least there'd be an APB out for the two men now. That call had been made.

Beth jabbed the button for the fourth floor twice more in a futile attempt to speed up the ride. Not that he blamed her. He feared if he didn't sit down soon, he was going to fall down. But after everything that had happened today, he wasn't letting Beth see him as weak.

He rested his uninjured shoulder against the fake cherrywood wall of the elevator and stared at the poster of a grinning hotel employee plastered to the door, the seam cutting neatly down the middle of her face, widening her nose.

Beth followed his gaze. "What were they thinking?"

Corbin smiled. "It's gonna get worse when the door opens."

With her guard down, there was an alluring, engaging quality about Beth that sent warmth radiating through his chest. Nothing with this case had gone as planned. He'd become accustomed to a certain level of predictability. He'd become accustomed to trusting his instincts. Beth had him second-guessing everything. When she'd purchased a false identity, he'd made an assumption.

His feelings for her had clouded his thinking.

Believing she was guilty had put some distance between them. Distance he obviously needed.

They reached the fourth floor, and the bell sounded. The smiling picture on the door split in two.

They both laughed and the tension of the past few hours seeped from his bones, leaving only weary resignation. He couldn't change the past. He couldn't undo his mistake. He could avoid making more. Beth was part of the case. She was off-limits. Since she didn't appear to return his regard, staying away should be easy.

Their footsteps were muffled over carpet patterned in rust-colored geometric shapes. Decorative sconces cast star-shaped patterns over the dappled wallpaper.

She glanced at the number on the door and paused. "I'm 404, and you're 406."

He clutched his room card, his hand hovering over the handle. "You all right for a few hours?"

She'd had an eventful day, to say the least. According to his many army debriefings, she needed time alone to process the events. Whatever that meant.

"I'll be fine." She glanced at the bag dangling from her fingertips and jolted. "I almost forgot. I bought us a couple of toiletry sets from the drugstore. There was a male version and a female version." She plucked a plastic, floral patterned bag from the sack. "This one is mine."

"Thank you." He hoped there was a razor in there. His chin itched. As she stifled a yawn, Corbin looped the bag over his fingers. "Then everything else in here is mine?"

"Yep." Her nostrils flared, and she fought back another yawn. "The medical supplies and stuff." She waved her card before the lock and waited for the click, then toed open the door. "It's nearly 2:00 a.m. I'm so tired, I'm afraid I'm going to start hallucinating. Don't worry, though. I have a little stamina left. Give me a minute, and I'll come around to bandage that for you."

Corbin shook his head. "I don't need the help. Thanks, anyway."

"It's no trouble." She retracted her foot and closed the distance between them. "I don't mind."

"You're exhausted." He stepped into his room and faced her. "Get some rest."

As gently as he could, he let the door close. It wasn't her responsibility to care for him. The responsibility rested the other way around.

Corbin staggered back a few steps and collapsed on to the bed. He splayed his arms and stared at the ceiling. The next few hours were going to be the true test. Short of locking her in the neighboring room, he was at a loss.

Would she stay, or would she run? He was one

man operating alone. He was wounded. If he turned her over to the police, she'd be targeted with the false embezzling charges. If he turned her over to the FBI, they'd dangle her as bait— neither of which seemed any safer than what he was offering. At least this way they were operating off the grid.

Until the email arrived, everything was speculation. Her story seemed far-fetched, at best. Even to him.

The ceiling wavered, and his vision blurred from exhaustion.

"Fine," she called through the door. "Die in there for all I care."

"Good night, Beth."

He didn't have much at stake. Just his entire career.

Beth stepped back and huffed. She did care. She cared very much.

Grumbling, she returned to her room. After brushing her teeth and washing her face, she paced before the two double beds.

She glanced at her bag and did a double take. How were they being tracked? Corbin was convinced she was the cause—albeit unintentionally. He'd insisted she abandon her belongings, but she hadn't gotten rid of *everything*. She'd been so certain of herself—what if she was wrong?

After dumping the contents on to the comforter, she dug out her dad's picture. She'd considered the frame too small and thin to be able to hide anything, but what did she know? She didn't exactly have a subscription to *Spy Magazine Weekly*.

The frame was wooden, but not expensive, and the seams were attached with heavy, sharp staples. She pried them apart and searched every inch of the frame. Nothing. Her shoulders sagged as she exhaled her pent-up breath. No telltale spy chips. No sign of tampering.

She pressed the frame back together as best she could. The pieces didn't quite match up after the abuse. She'd buy a new one when everything settled down. At least one thing hadn't gone wrong today. She didn't want to have that conversation with Corbin.

Oh, sorry, it was my fault we were being chased all along. No hard feelings, right?

Corbin.

The stubborn idiot.

There was no way he could bandage the arm on his own. She had a feeling he was testing her. Seeing what she'd do. Would she contact someone? Would she run? It would serve him right if she disappeared into the night. But she was staying. She'd made her decision.

He wasn't going to ask for her help. She had to take matters into her own hands.

"Let me in." She knocked on the adjoining door, and called, "You can't reach that shoulder by yourself."

"Go to sleep, Beth," came the muted reply.

She paced before the closed door and grumbled. He'd bleed to death rather than admit he needed help. She sat on the edge of the bed and crossed her legs, then crossed her arms. She flexed the ankle of her dangling foot a few times before springing to her feet.

She took the stairs two at a time and retrieved another key card from the sharp-eyed desk clerk. A benefit of being the one who'd checked them in earlier, both rooms were under her assumed name. Returning to their adjoining suites, she knocked gently on his door.

When he didn't answer, she used the key card.

Keeping one eye squinted, she peered around the edge of the door.

"I hope you're decent," she called quietly.

Corbin glared at her from his seat on the nearest double bed. A five o'clock shadow darkened his chin, and the bruise on his jaw had swelled and turned purple. He'd yanked his shirt sleeve over his shoulder and held a square of gauze against the wound. Deep red blood seeped through the cracks in his fingers.

She tsked. "You started the bleeding again, didn't you?"

His vivid blue eyes drooped to red slits. "It's better than it looks."

"I'm going to get some ice for that chin." She stepped through the doorway and grasped the plastic-lined ice bucket from the side table. "Don't bleed to death before I get back."

He scowled in reply.

She returned a short time later and pressed the makeshift ice pack against his jaw.

He covered her hand with his, holding the bag in place, and offered a reluctant, "Thank you."

"You're welcome." She brushed aside a dark lock of hair trapped beneath the frame of his glasses. The strands were surprisingly soft, and her fingers lingered. Though she doubted he'd ever admit as much, he was exhausted. "You really should engage the slide bolt when you're in a hotel room. You never know what sort of people are lurking around the corridors."

"I wasn't worried." He grunted. "I figured you'd be long gone by now."

She snatched her hand away.

He *had* been testing her. "Then why do you look annoyed that I'm still here, instead of relieved?"

"Because you should be getting some sleep," he said. "We've got an early start tomorrow."

They were *both* exhausted and cranky—an ominous combination. She should have let him bleed out alone. But there was more than one stubborn person in the room.

"After you slammed the door in my face, I considered doing just that." Guilt tripped along her nerve endings. "Except I didn't trust you to take care of that wound alone."

There was nothing stopping her from leaving, and despite the parking garage, she hadn't ruled out Corbin as the one being tracked. Even with her misgivings, she couldn't fathom abandoning him when he was injured.

The supplies they'd purchased earlier were strewn over the harvest-gold flocked bedspread. Bandages, gauze and butterfly strips were set alongside antibacterial ointment.

She tore open one of the boxes. "Lie down."

He peeled the gauze aside, and she caught her first real look at the damage inflicted by the gunshot.

Blinking rapidly, she kept her expression carefully neutral. The wound was two inches long and ugly, the edges jagged. A crimson-soaked towel rested on the bed beside him. Her stomach pitched, and she took a deep, calming breath through her nose.

"Does it hurt?" she asked.

He swallowed, and his Adam's apple worked. "Not much."

"Men," she muttered. "You said this was a scratch."

"It is."

She pressed the back of her hand to his forehead, and he flinched away. She held up her arms in a placating gesture. "Easy there, superhero. I'm just checking to see if you're running a fever. You don't feel warm. That's something."

"Sorry," he said sheepishly. "It's been a long day."

"You're telling me." She gently nudged him, being careful to avoid the wound, and gestured toward the pillow. "This will go much faster and easier if you don't argue with me."

Their gazes met and clashed, and they engaged in a silent war of wills. He was bigger and stronger, and she had no authority over him. She sensed he was accustomed to giving the orders, and not receiving them. So was she. After a long moment, his expression softened.

"Fine," he said, his voice hoarse—almost pained. "But make it quick. It doesn't have to be pretty. We both need sleep."

She offered a half grin. "Yes, sir."

He rested his head against his pillow and tucked his fingers under his cheek, then lifted his legs on to the coverlet. He used his right hand to hold the ice pack against his jaw. She sat and adjusted the light before leaning in.

He appeared younger, almost boyish, and her heart went out to him. What was he like as a child? What forces had shaped him? As much as he played the tough guy, he was never overbearing or forceful. He'd even apologized at the train station for pretending to be her boyfriend. He'd only been trying to warn her. How could she fault him for trying to save her life?

She was grateful he'd been thinking on his feet. He'd been focused on her safety even though she was technically in his custody. Were it not for his quick action, things might have gone very differently for her.

She owed him. Whatever happened in the future, they were compelled to work together now. They might as well make the best of it.

"You really need stitches," she said. "I can pull the edges together, but you're going to have a scar."

His strained face was set against the pain he was experiencing. "Won't be the first. Let's just get this over with."

She dabbed a pad soaked with antibacterial ointment around the edges of the wound. "This is going to hurt."

"Yep."

"I thought the Feds were morning people," she cajoled.

"It's not morning, it's the middle of the night." He hissed, his lips tightening across his teeth. "I seem to recall someone else saying that."

"At least you haven't lost your sense of humor." His expression was pinched, and she sympathized with his predicament. "You really need a doctor and not an accountant with a first aid badge from summer camp."

"That's better than nothing." He took off his glasses and placed them on the nightstand. "I thought you were a forensic accountant."

She caught herself staring and glanced away. She'd never seen him without his glasses. While some people might prefer his looks this way, unimpeded, she liked the glasses.

Her heart did a little zigzag in her chest. She liked the handsome, Clark Kent appeal.

After donning the disposable gloves, she cleaned the wound with the supplies she'd bought, then used the butterfly bandages to hold the edges together. He must despise being out of control and dependent, but he remained silent during her ministrations, barely flinching.

She carefully washed the area around the wound in small circles, then rinsed and patted his skin dry with a fresh towel.

"I have a confession," she said, smiling.

He seemed to read the amusement in her eyes. "What's that?"

"I exaggerated my summer camp merit badge."

"How so?"

"The badge was for first aid rendered to a stuffed animal. I administered aid to my teddy bear."

"Did he survive?"

"To a ripe old age."

"Then you earned your badge."

She'd never been a particularly nurturing person. Maybe because she'd been raised by her dad, or maybe it was just her inherent personality. Either way, she'd never been one to bandage up her dolls as a child. She'd been more interested in reading. Yet caring for Corbin was invoking feelings she'd never experienced before.

As she smoothed the bandage, she caught sight of a scar slashing across his forearm.

She touched the spot. "What's this from?"

He observed her from lowered lids as her fingers paused. Goose bumps pebbled his arm.

"Shrapnel," he said without elaborating.

She'd been around enough cops growing up to know there were all kinds of heroes. Willing and unwilling, tragic and flawed. There were braggarts and loners. Even if he'd rescued a classroom full of small children and a litter of puppies from a burning building, she had no doubt he'd downplay the tale. There was an inherent protectiveness about him.

She'd watched him over the past two weeks, and there were certain qualities that stood out. While she realized he'd been acting, no one could change their nature entirely. There was an unconscious selflessness about him. An automatic need to look out for those around him. She'd seen this character trait during meetings, and she'd seen him in action when danger swirled around them.

Her hands fidgeted with the bedspread. "When I asked before, you said that you served in the military."

"Yep."

"Special Forces?"

"Something like that."

"Humph." She perched next to him, stretched out her legs and flexed her feet. "Has anyone ever told you that you're a wonderful conversationalist?"

He set the ice pack on the nightstand. "Nope."

"Didn't think so."

He sat up and swung his legs over the side of the bed. His head was bent, and he braced his hands against the mattress. She made a point of gathering the supplies, her gaze averted.

She was pestering him, but she didn't see the harm. He'd investigated her, after all. It was only fair, considering the circumstances, that she knew a little bit more about him.

Shouldn't she be allowed some information about the man who held her life in his hands? The only thing that had been standing between her and certain death at that train station had been

Corbin. She'd have walked right into the arms of that goon if he hadn't been there to stop her.

"You can't blame me for being curious." She heaved a sigh. "It's nearly three in the morning. I've been shot at and nearly kidnapped. Twice. I'm exhausted, but I don't feel like I can sleep. I haven't been up this late since I was cramming for tests as an undergraduate."

She'd reached that odd state of exhaustion where she felt as though she'd tipped over a precipice. Her thoughts were fuzzy and unfocused, ricocheting around her head. The tension of the past few weeks had left her drained and mentally weak. She wanted a friend. She wanted someone to confide in. She wanted to talk to her dad.

She missed being completely authentic with someone. In all friendships, everyone played a role, and she'd always been the boring, responsible friend. When everyone else was acting crazy around her, she'd felt as though she was oil floating on water. She'd see their drama, but she was never pulled in. Now she was caught in a hurricane, and she couldn't slow down long enough to catch her bearings.

"You've been through a lot today," Corbin said. "It's understandable. The adrenaline is still wearing off for me, too. You'll sleep for a week when this is all over. Trust me, exhaustion has a way of catching up with you when you least expect it."

He spoke like someone who was intimately familiar with the effects, and she suddenly understood why friendships forged under tense circumstances were the friends one kept for life. Bonds formed under stress were durable. Tested.

The room suddenly became too small, and the air too close. "At least the shot didn't graze your other arm," she said with a weary smile. "Karli, from accounting, would be devastated if anything happened to that tattoo." Keeping her gaze averted, she gathered the garbage into the discarded plastic bag. He'd tossed his suit jacket on the bed, and she touched the torn sleeve, instantly yanked back to the moment on the platform. "I was terrified when I heard that gunshot."

The words seemed to trigger a relaxing of her guard against the fear and shock, and she fought against weakening. She desperately needed those defenses in place if she was going to survive the next few days.

"You were supposed to be running in the opposite direction," he said pointedly.

The shaking began again, like it had earlier in the car. Or was it yesterday? She'd lost all track of time and place. Her body seemed to have a will of its own.

To cover her reaction, she said, "It's a good thing I didn't run."

She'd taken control of the situation. When she'd

seen Corbin on the ground, seen the man reaching for the gun, she'd known she had to act. A violent shudder traveled all the way down her body.

She was tired of being scared. She wanted another emotion. Anger. Frustration. Joy. Anything but this constant dread.

They sat side by side, though not touching, and warmth radiated from his body. Her gaze lingered on his lips, and her pulse thrummed.

For a moment she thought he swayed toward her. Butterflies floated in her stomach. She jolted to her feet.

What was she doing? She barely knew him. She'd worked with him for two weeks, and she didn't know which parts of his personality were the truth, and which parts were a lie.

Corbin coughed quietly and sat up straighter. The moment had passed. Instead of feeling relieved, she felt vaguely empty. As though she'd missed out on forming a deeper connection with someone and might never get another chance.

He adjusted the bandage and said, "Thanks for helping," without looking up.

"It's the least I could do. You saved my life twice, remember?"

He rolled back the sleeve on his left arm, and she finally got a chance to view the elaborate tattoo on his arm. There were loops and whirls, the pattern geometrical, almost Aztec-looking in design.

She tilted her head. "What does all that mean?"

"It means I was young and stupid once." He rubbed his fingertips over his creased brow. "I lost someone, and I went a little crazy. Did some dumb stuff. I'm stuck with it now."

"In Afghanistan?"

"Yep." He stared at the patterns on his arm as though seeing them for the first time. "It's embarrassing now, but it seemed like the thing to do at the time."

"I think it's understandable. Grief does odd things to people. I wish we could go back to Victorian times when people wore black armbands to show they were in mourning. Like a warning to others. Beware—this person may burst into tears at any moment. I was a mess after my dad died."

"I'm sorry. I saw his picture on your desk. He must have passed away young. Did he die in the line of duty?"

"No. He would have loved that, though."

"I shouldn't have—"

"Don't apologize. That came out all wrong. It's just that he loved the job, and he would have liked to die doing something spectacular. He would have enjoyed the rest of his buddies having a drink and telling increasing taller tales about him. Instead, he had a stroke. He spent the last few months of his life trapped in his own body. He couldn't talk. He couldn't feed himself." She made a sound of frustration. "You must think I'm a total basket case discussing this with you. We don't even know each other, and you want to arrest me."

"I don't—"

"Never mind. It's all right. What does it matter? It's not like we'll ever see each other after this. When my dad died, I was like a raw nerve ending." She knotted the plastic bag around her fingers. The talking seemed to help. She'd kept everything inside for so long. There was a part of her that desperately wanted Corbin to understand something about her. She wanted *someone* to understand. "I felt every emotion so deeply. I'd never been like that before. I'd always been cool and analytical. Not then. Everything was exaggerated. I wasn't angry at injustice. I was enraged. I wasn't frustrated by the traffic. I was infuriated. I cried during all the holiday commercials, especially the one where the soldier surprises his family on Christmas morning. And it wasn't even the sad stuff. I once laughed so hard at a joke that I snorted during a business dinner. I'm sure my friends thought I was going mad. Getting a tattoo doesn't seem that strange to me."

"At least you can wear what you want at work." He nudged her with his elbow. "Because of most dress codes, I have to wear long sleeves, no matter the weather."

"I think it makes you look dangerous. In a good way."

"A good way, huh," he said. "At least you didn't do any permanent damage."

"Not completely permanent, thankfully." She stared at her hands. "Remember when you asked why I left my first job? The relationship gone wrong? I was so blind. So stupid back then."

"What happened?"

Maybe if he knew the truth, he wouldn't look at her with such suspicion in his eyes. The company had swept the mess under the rug. They'd all scuttled away like cockroaches when someone turned on the light.

"His name was Brian. He was a rising star in the company. Youngest ever CFO. He was handsome and charming. He was also cooking the books to hide the fact that the company wasn't growing as fast as projected."

Unloading the truth felt like releasing an incredible burden. She'd seen the signs, but she'd made excuses for him. She'd given Brian a chance to tell the truth, but he'd only sunk deeper into his lies. If he'd confided in her, she would have helped him. If he'd accepted his punishment, she'd have stood by him. If he'd admitted he'd made a mistake, she'd have forgiven him. But somewhere along the line he'd convinced himself that he deserved the money. There was always a point, in any fraud, when people decided the law didn't apply to them.

"Let me guess," Corbin said. "He also skimmed a little off the top for himself."

"You guessed right." She barked out a humorless laugh. "He tried to convince me that we'd both be considered guilty. That I should cover for him. Only he wasn't smart enough to cover his tracks in the first place. He certainly wasn't smart enough to frame someone else." She stared at her hands. "After I turned him in, they asked for my resignation."

"Bad publicity?"

She turned her quizzical gaze on him. "Yep. Wanted to erase all the reminders of what had happened." Corbin seemed to understand how the business worked. "Then you understand why I had to do what I did."

"And you have to understand, as well. This is my job. We've been over this. You were the one person who'd been linked to Cayman Holdings in both cases. Even you must see the connection."

"No matter what they told you, I was a good employee. I did what I thought was right. If I'd let Brian get away with what he'd done, he'd have exploited another company. That's what happens. Instead of being punished, bad employees are shuffled from one company to another to avoid embarrassment. In my line of work, I see it more than anyone. I stand by my decision."

"You were right." He paused. "I do owe you an apology. There was no blemish on your record. Merely a note that you'd left abruptly. I was fishing. Trying to see if there was anything else at work."

Relief shuddered through her. "Now you know the truth."

"I'm sorry about what happened." He sighed. "People can be incredibly disappointing."

She had a feeling he was thinking of a very specific person. *Her.* Yet she'd done nothing wrong. All she'd ever wanted to do was turn over the evidence without winding up in the morgue. She might have turned a blind eye. She'd be asleep in Chicago. She hadn't. She couldn't.

"Don't get me wrong." She tipped her head and stared at the popcorn ceiling. "I think Brian liked me. Maybe even loved me, in his own way. He thought I loved him enough to hide what he was doing. He was wrong."

Corbin's gaze grew intense. "And you never considered looking the other way?"

"Never. Probably sounds stupid, but I was raised on truth and justice." She ducked her head and reached in her pocket. "Here's the extra key card."

Exhaustion was turning her batty. She was losing herself all over again—her resistance was down. She was adrift from everything that made her who she was—her name, her home, her work. Even her new clothing felt itchy and wrong. She craved a connection, something familiar and comforting.

"Beth," he said.

"Yes."

"I don't think anyone else could have held up as well as you have."

"Thank you." A flush of heat crept up her neck. She wasn't expecting his compliment. "You need to have that cut checked by a professional. If there's any sign of infection. Any at all, we'll have to risk visiting a clinic."

She still had a chance to follow her original plan. She didn't want anyone else to get hurt. Least of all, Corbin. It was like Timothy all over again. She'd set this chain of events into motion, and it was her job to work out the difficulties.

Truth and justice were an illusion. She'd wanted to believe that good conquered evil. Her dad had encouraged the myth. He must have known the truth all along. Fighting injustice was an uphill, losing battle.

How did she untangle this mess without involving anyone else?

"A bit of advice," Corbin said, sitting up straighter.

"Mmm-hmm?"

"I think you're telling the truth, but I won't

know for sure until the email. Which means I also can't stop you if you decide to leave tonight. But if you run, I will find you. And if I discover you're involved, I'll prosecute you to the full extent of the law."

And just like that—her benevolent mood evaporated. All the exhaustion she'd been feeling flew away. That's what she got for confiding in the man who thought she was laundering money for terrorists.

"I'm not the only one who got shot at tonight." Her exhaustion had taken on a life of its own. She felt as though she'd separated from her body, and she was standing on the outside looking in on herself. "Did it ever occur to you that you might be wrong? I can disappear faster on my own. Maybe you're the one who led those two men to me."

He shook his head. "Did you ever consider the legal trouble you're courting? I'm assuming a forensic accountant needs a higher level of trust than most other professionals. What happens if you come up in an internet search under suspicion of using a false identity? What if Quetech accuses you of stealing corporate secrets and we can't prove you're a whistle-blower? If that email doesn't show up on Tuesday, it's going to be even worse for you. Consider what you do next very carefully."

In that instant, his words felt like the ultimate betrayal.

He didn't trust her. He never would. She'd done what she thought was right on both occasions, and she'd gotten burned twice. What was the point of doing the right thing?

Trust was a fantasy. Moral bravery was a fairy tale told from a church pulpit. All anyone cared about was the bottom line. Greed always won. She might as well be tilting at windmills for all the good she was doing.

She hadn't gotten the world and she'd still lost her soul. Her dad should have given her another Biblical quote. His favorite wasn't working.

"Then you don't trust me," she said.

"I don't trust myself."

Her blood went from a simmer to a boil in a flash. "After everything I've done for you today, you still don't believe I'm innocent?"

He rubbed the back of his neck. "I know you didn't have anything to do with Sam's death."

"But you're not certain about my involvement in the money laundering?"

"It's my job to be suspicious. This will all be cleared up when your email arrives. Until then, you're better off with me. Stick with being the real Beth Greenwood."

"That's rich, coming from you. What is that like? Seeing everyone as a corrupt?" She refused to moderate the shrill edge in voice. "You spent two weeks watching me. Spying on me! For all I know, you've been keeping track of me for the last two years. What is it like, suspecting that everyone you meet is deceiving you when all the while it's you who's lying?"

"You tell me, Beth. Why didn't you ask someone for help?" His voice took on a steely edge. "Your dad was a cop, after all. Why didn't you at least go to the police? Why don't you trust anyone?"

"We've been over this. Homeland Security and the FBI couldn't protect Timothy Swan. I didn't trust them to protect me."

"We didn't know then what we know now. You don't think we're smart enough to put different protocols in place?"

If he hadn't interfered, she'd be on the California Zephyr, enjoying a sandwich and watching the scenery. Acting independently was the only surefire way to know she wasn't being deceived.

"You have no right to lecture me about trust," she said at last.

That was the worst part—knowing he'd only been nice to her for the past two weeks because he wanted something. He was no different than Brian. She was a means to an end, not a person.

To think she'd even considered his invitation to coffee with any sincerity. If she hadn't been trying to make a speedy getaway, she might have considered watching karaoke with him. Even after Brian, she was still the same trusting fool with bad instincts.

You'd think after all this time she'd have learned.

"Listen to me, Beth," Corbin said, taking the key card from her limp hand. "I only have your best interests at heart. I'm trying to help you."

"Really? Or are you trying to help yourself? Your career?"

A flash of guilt streaked across his features before he quickly schooled his expression. The betrayal slammed into her chest.

A memory jogged its way to the forefront. Quetech had been celebrating the September birthdays and anniversaries. One of those awkward events that she was uncomfortable attending. Yet she'd learned over the years that sitting at her desk only invited more attention. She'd been hovering in the doorway, ready to make an escape, when Corbin had caught her eye and waved her over.

She'd felt a camaraderie with him. A kinship. At the time, she'd thought she'd found an ally. A couple of newbies supporting each other. That was the worst part. Knowing that after all this time, she was still the same gullible fool falling for the same old manipulations.

He rested the extra key card on the nightstand. "This will all be finished soon enough."

They were both exhausted and out of sorts. She sensed he was lashing out at her, but she didn't know why. People were dying. Timothy. Sam. For what? So someone could set off a bomb and kill innocent people to make a point? What a waste.

She stood and tossed his bag of supplies next to the key card. "You'll just have to wait and find out if I'm here in the morning, won't you?"

He already thought the worst of her, what was the point in trying to change his mind?

SEVEN

Corbin welcomed the distracting pain as he dressed on Saturday. He owed Beth an apology. If she'd stuck around.

He smoothed the bandage on his arm and flexed his fingers. She'd done excellent work dressing his injury considering she was an accountant and not an EMT.

Sitting next to her, his defenses weakened by hours on high alert, he'd actually thought about kissing her. The idea had seemed so natural at the time, almost inevitable—though he'd suffer the consequences both personally and professionally later. She was under his protection, and even the idea of taking advantage of her vulnerability made him the worst sort of jerk.

Bracing one hand against the sink, he stared at the patterned tile floor. How would he explain that to Baker? *Well, boss, I was tired, and I've been thinking about her a lot the past few weeks.*

She has the most beautiful green eyes, and she smells exquisite.

At best he'd receive a rebuke, at worst he'd be out of a job.

He splashed cold water on his face and sipped the weak brew the tiny coffeemaker had produced. He'd washed out his bloodied clothes, but there was no disguising the tears in the sleeves of his shirt and coat. After donning his jacket, he slipped from the room. At half past seven in the morning, the hotel corridor was deserted.

He'd placed a snare to see if Beth had left during the night. As he crouched to check the spot, an unexpected surge of adrenaline jolted through him. He caught sight of the strip of medical tape near the bottom of the door and heaved a sigh.

She'd stayed.

His arm ached, and he rolled his shoulder a few times. Despite the throbbing pain, he'd managed to sleep for a few hours. He functioned well with limited amounts of rest; a skill left over from his military days.

He doubted Beth had the same endurance— she'd been a nervous wreck the previous day, and probably hadn't slept much in the past week. Instead of waking her, he slipped a hastily scrawled note beneath her door telling her he'd be back soon.

He lingered a moment before pivoting on his

heel. She had every right to be angry with him. She'd confided in him last evening, and he'd shoved her trust back in her face with his accusations. He didn't know why he'd done it; he only knew he couldn't seem to think straight when he was around her.

Who was he fooling? He knew exactly why he'd pushed her away. He'd pushed her away because she trusted him. She was under his protection. He was afraid if she let him kiss her, he'd have to acknowledge his feelings.

He was attracted to her. Drawn to her sharp wit and keen intelligence. He sensed she liked him, too. A little. When he wasn't acting like a jerk.

Forgoing the elevator, he took the stairs to the lobby. He found the business center and surfed through the local advertisements on the hotel computer until he discovered what he was looking for, then visited the ATM and withdrew the maximum allotted cash. He'd make do for now.

He checked the time and decided to kill another hour while Beth slept. He returned to the computer and did a few searches.

She'd left her previous job because of a failed relationship. He'd seen a name on her file, and now he was curious.

Brian Wilkins, the most likely candidate to be her previous boyfriend, was a former CFO of Tri-Court Industries who'd spent sixteen months in federal prison for embezzlement and falsifying records. He'd been ordered to pay restitution, but an investigator calculated that the company had only recovered half of the missing funds. Corbin scrolled through a few more screens. According to his hometown newspaper, Brian had decided to see the world from a sailboat upon his release.

Corbin grunted. Figured. People who embezzled money bought boats and disappeared. Beth was better off without the loser.

Glancing at the clock, he decided to read the complimentary newspaper he'd grabbed from the tall stack and did the crossword puzzle in ink—only crossing out one mistake. The clerk was the same young man who'd been there the previous evening, and the two shared a commiserating look as Corbin tossed the newspaper into the recycle bin.

He took the steps two at a time to the fourth floor before deciding to go all the way to the top. When he reached the ladder to the roof, he jogged to the bottom floor and repeated the maneuver twice more. The exercise got his blood pumping, and he was feeling almost normal by the time he returned to his room.

As he passed Beth's door, his gaze snagged on a dangling piece of white tape. His pulse jumped. The marker was missing. He knocked on the door and held his ear closer. Nothing. He didn't have a key to her room, but there was the adjoining door between them.

His ears buzzed. Turning the latch slowly, he pressed open the door to his room. Nothing appeared disturbed or out of place.

How much time had his exercise on the stairwell taken? Fifteen minutes. Maybe twenty at the most. There was a chance someone had grabbed her while he jogged the stairs, but he doubted it. Not without causing a commotion.

Still, he kept his movements silent as he passed through his room. He drew his gun before testing the knob. She hadn't set the bolt. The door swung open with a squeak.

He sensed the room was deserted even before he stepped over the threshold. Empty spaces had a distinctive, hollow feel to them.

The room appeared pristine. Untouched. As though housekeeping had just exited. Perplexed, he hovered on the threshold. The bed was made with crisp precision. As though it had never been slept in. He half expected to see a wrapped mint on the fluffed pillows, but the hotel wasn't that luxurious.

He lowered his gun to his side. She hadn't left after their conversation the previous evening— the marker had been in place earlier. Maybe she'd caught a few hours of sleep before slipping past him in the lobby.

He couldn't say she hadn't warned him.

Annoyance tripped along the edges of his exhaustion. She wouldn't get very far this time—not with an APB out for her arrest. He'd also made a note of the alias she was using when she secured their rooms the previous evening.

Holstering his gun, he nudged open the door to the bathroom. The pink floral bag of toiletries rested on the counter. A single towel had been hung out to dry.

Corbin scratched his temple. Why leave the supplies she'd purchased only last night? His note was perched on the top of the trash.

As he contemplated the bathroom, the room door swung open. He flattened his back against the wall and peered through the crack.

Beth stepped into the room, a tray of food in her outstretched hands.

He waited until she'd safely set down her burden before loudly clearing his throat as he stepped from the bathroom.

She shrieked and stumbled backward. "You scared me to death." She pressed her hand over her heart. "What were you doing lurking in there?"

"I, um, you didn't answer when I knocked." He stared at the patterned rug. "I was worried."

"Really?" She crossed her arms and drummed her fingers on her biceps. "Or did you think I'd run and you were searching my room?"

He shifted from foot to foot. "Looks like you found the complimentary breakfast buffet."

"That's not an answer." She huffed and waved her hand over the tray. "There wasn't much selection, but I got a little bit of everything."

"You did mention that you might not be here today."

"Only to annoy you."

"It worked." He accepted the second cup of coffee on the tray, his hand surprisingly steady. "Thank you. This is much better than what I managed to squeeze from that tiny little coffee machine they leave in the room."

"You're babbling. Be careful. I think a part of you might actually want to trust me."

Regret sat heavy in the pit of his stomach. He hadn't only annoyed her the previous evening, he'd hurt her. He'd been exhausted, the pain clouding his judgment. He'd been looking for signs of guilt instead of looking for signs of innocence up until seconds ago. If what she said was true, then she'd taken a terrible risk for no discernable payoff.

It had been easier to believe she was running, motivated by greed or even fear over what she'd done. For someone to take that sort of responsibility for no gain had seemed unfathomable.

The facts fit both scenarios. Either she'd done something terrible, and she was trying to escape

the consequences. Or she'd done something incredibly brave at great personal risk. The more he
knew her, the more he feared the latter was true.

By ignoring the idea that she might be innocent, he'd ignored the pieces of the puzzle that
supported her innocence.

Her dad had been a cop. A good cop. A clean
cop, by all accounts. A man who'd dedicated his
life to the job. A widower who'd raised his only
daughter by himself. Raised his daughter to live
by the same rigid set of moral codes he'd set for
himself.

Near as she could tell, all she wanted out of this
whole mess was to live to see another sunrise.

No wonder she was annoyed with him. "I
may have jumped to the wrong conclusion when
you didn't answer my knock," he conceded. "I
apolo—"

"No. You're right." She sighed and reached for
a paper cup of orange juice. "I didn't give you
any reason to believe I'd stick around. I think the
lack of sleep was making me a little crazy. Can
we just—can we just forget everything I said last
night?"

She was innocent.

He knew it then. Knew it to his bones. Everything fell too neatly into place.

She hadn't been manipulating him. She'd confided in him. She'd shown him a part of herself,

and he'd shut her out. He'd miscalculated, and that miscalculation was going to cost him dearly.

She'd reached out for his trust, and he'd slammed the door on her overture. She wasn't going to be as forthright in the future. Building her trust once more was going to take a great deal of time and effort.

Time was a commodity he didn't have. "Don't apologize for anything that's happened. None of this is your fault. None of this is my fault. If people followed the letter of the law, we'd both be out of a job."

"True," she said. "I'm feeling much more charitable after getting some sleep. I wasn't myself last night."

She seemed in good spirits, and he decided not to press her. He'd made enough missteps. It was time to back off. Give her a little breathing space. He was starting to wonder if he was cut out for this line of work. Beth was testing all the assumptions he had about himself.

"There's a table in my room." He lifted the tray. "Why don't we eat in there?"

"My room doesn't have a table. I should have paid more attention last night." She disappeared and returned a moment later with her pink floral bag. "Do you mind if I brush my teeth in your sink? The faucet in my room doesn't have any water pressure."

"Suit yourself."

She snatched her supplies from the sink and returned a moment later. He held open the door with his hip and let her pass. She'd taken a shower, and her hair had mostly dried. The damp strands were wavy and curled at the ends. His heart kicked in his chest. He much preferred the casual style to her severe bun. At work she was buttoned up and standoffish. He hadn't seen this more approachable side of her.

Hovering on the threshold, he glanced between the two rooms with a frown. Neither of them had left a single trace of themselves. Granted, they were traveling light. Yet they'd both made the bed with military precision, the pillows arranged just so. Two people forcing order into a chaotic world. Maybe that's why they rubbed each other the wrong way.

They had too much in common.

He let the adjoining door swing shut behind them and click into place.

She pulled out a chair and snatched a slice of bacon from one of the plates. "The same clerk from last night was still on duty this morning. He's working a double shift. I didn't want to appear too shady, so I told him a couple of coworkers might be looking for me. I figured that was less suspicious than telling him two goons were chasing us. Anyway, he said no one had asked about us last night or this morning. He also said he wasn't allowed to give anyone our room numbers, and he'd call if someone asked about us."

Corbin hadn't even considered questioning the clerk. Maybe because he didn't trust anyone. He saw everyone as a threat. "Good idea."

"I should check your arm."

He flexed his fingers. "It's fine."

"All right." Her voice was tight. "What now?"

He mentally kicked himself once again. He'd just passed up another opportunity to rebuild some trust between them. There were times when his training in Afghanistan was a hindrance. In his former line of work, he'd always been on the defensive.

He hadn't been part of the community outreach. He hadn't been trained to build trust. He'd been trained to view everything and everyone as a danger.

That method wasn't working out so well these days.

He took a plate holding a surprisingly large omelet oozing with cheese. "I've found a car for sale at a small dealership. It's old, but apparently it runs great, and the dealership is open this morning. I don't want to risk a cyber trail with a rental. Airplanes mean identification, and I'd rather avoid that, as well." Just in case they picked up Beth. He wasn't worried about himself. "After we find a car, we'll drive to headquarters. Without current license plates, we're relatively obscure."

"How far is headquarters?"

"About eleven hundred miles."

"What happened to Minneapolis?"

"My superior thinks headquarters is safer. We'll follow part of the plan, at least. Go someplace public, make sure we don't still have a tail, then make the trip by car."

Her expression fell. "You have got to be kidding me. Are you certain we can't take a plane?"

"We can take the bus," he said cheerfully. "That's what Jack Reacher always does. He takes the bus to stay off the grid. You don't need identification. But I don't think you're going to enjoy that mode of transportation any better."

"Agreed. I do not want to be stuck on a bus for twenty hours. What a nightmare. What about the train?" Her voice raised in hope. "The train was nice."

"They already know you have a proclivity for train travel."

"I suppose you're right. Maybe I'll catch up on some reading. Can we stop at a bookstore?"

"When it's safe."

Though he was confident they hadn't been followed from the train station, he wasn't letting down his guard until they were back at Homeland Security headquarters.

They spent the next fifteen minutes talking about general topics. Light, innocuous conversation. They both had a weakness for action movies. They both preferred cats to dogs. They were both avid readers, though Beth preferred young adult, and he devoured military fiction.

Sunlight streaming through the windows glinted off her hair and brought out the luster of her eyes. He felt her laughter to the very center of his being. That was the problem. They had too much drawing them together. Too much in common. It was a dangerous mix.

A noise from her room caught his attention and they both went quiet. The faint ringing of a phone echoed through the thin walls. The noise was coming from Beth's room. She half stood, and Corbin placed a restraining hand on her arm.

"Wait," he whispered. "That might be the front desk ringing to let you know someone is looking for you."

"Tweedledum and Tweedledumber?"

"Best guess."

The muscles beneath his fingers worked. "Then they already know we're here."

"Maybe," he said, his voice low. "If it's them, we'll keep them off balance. Guessing. Let's not give them any more information than we have to."

"All right," Beth whispered.

"Get your stuff together. If they're near the hotel, we have to be ready to move quickly."

Confusion and frustration warred within him. He'd been certain they were tracking Beth's phone. He'd been certain they'd lost the men downtown when they dumped their belongings. Then again, they didn't know who was calling Beth's room. Maybe it was the front desk. Maybe a wrong number. There was an infinite number of possibilities. No need to jump to conclusions.

Someone pounded on a nearby door, and Beth jerked around. "I think that's coming from my room. Someone's knocking."

The infinite number of possibilities immediately narrowed. "The phone call was a distraction."

The two men were in the building. He was certain of it.

Instantly alert, Corbin held his index finger before his lips. He motioned for Beth to move away from the door and drew his gun. Flattening himself against the wall, he angled his ear toward the seam in the adjoining door.

Muffled voices sounded from the opposite side. Male voices.

"They're here, all right," Corbin said quietly.

They were still being tracked. Though he couldn't see them, he knew they were the two men from the parking garage and the train station.

Corbin made a sound of frustration. If not her phone, then what? He trusted Baker, the only person on the inside who knew their whereabouts. He'd ditched his own phone. He'd even disassembled his Glock last night. While he'd kept the gun in his safe, there was a chance they'd been to his house. A chance they'd bypassed his alarm. Anything was possible.

He glanced at Beth. She carried everything she owned in a pink plastic pouch she'd purchased the previous evening.

He needed a wand to search for devices, but that meant contacting the authorities. Something he was rapidly reassessing.

He had to consider all the possibilities. Beth had gone downstairs to pick up breakfast. She could have called someone, but they'd have had to be practically waiting in the parking lot to arrive this fast. He didn't see how that was possible.

She threw back her shoulders and grasped her ball cap, then threaded her ponytail through the gap in the back. If she was lying, she was a wonderful actress. The best. She tugged on his sleeve and he lowered his head.

Her breath whispered over his ear, raising gooseflesh along his arms. "What do we do?"

"Get out of here," he replied grimly. "Fast."

The adjoining door was closed, but it hadn't been locked. How long before the men chasing them noticed, and decided to investigate? He jerked his head toward the exit. Beth nodded her understanding.

Careful not to make any noise, the two padded across the floor. As they passed the bathroom, Beth snatched the bag of toiletries and medical supplies from the sink.

The crinkling plastic sounded like a gunshot. She cringed and froze. Muffled thumps and the faint echo of voices continued from the other room. The adjoining door remained closed. Either the men hadn't heard them, or they weren't concerned about who was in the next room. Why should they be? They assumed he and Beth were together. They weren't considering they might have two rooms. Corbin blew out a silent breath and motioned again.

As he carefully opened the door, Beth hovered behind him. She kept one hand braced against his back. He was vitally aware of her—as though there was a magnetic pull between them. Her nose barely reached his shoulder blade, yet he sensed her whisper-soft breathing.

He angled his body and leaned closer to her ear. "We'll take the stairs. Move quick."

She reached for his hand, and he automatically clasped her fingers. All his instincts screamed her innocence. The proof was compelling. He was building trust. They were operating on the same side against the two men in the other room. He'd remain cautious, but she clearly didn't want to die any more than he did.

He was standing by his instincts. She was innocent. She was terrified.

He listened carefully. They were exposed for the twenty or so feet between here and the exit. Plenty of time to be spotted. A single door stood between them. The two men would see her room was undisturbed, and they weren't likely to linger.

He nodded. "Now."

Together they dashed for the door marked Exit. Once inside the stairwell, they jogged the floors and emerged into the lobby. Beth took a step into the open, and Corbin held her back. But not before the hotel clerk with the sharp eyes caught sight of them. A slight frown marred his expressive features. Corbin gave a shake of his head, hoping the young man read the gesture correctly.

"Let's wait here," Corbin said. "And make sure they've left."

He wasn't risking an ambush. Not alone.

"Okay."

His pulse picked up speed, and Corbin glanced between the exit and the clerk. Would the young man give them away? There was a fifty-fifty shot he hadn't understood the unspoken instructions.

The elevator doors opened with a ding, and Corbin urged Beth around the corner. They remained in the shadows, their bodies close enough he noted the tiny pulse beating gently in the hollow of her neck. She grasped a handful of his coat, her fingers trembling, and he wrapped an arm around her shoulders. His chest tightened.

If anyone passed by, they'd appear a loving couple sharing a clinch in the shadows.

She leaned into his embrace, and her soft hair brushed against his cheek. His breathing grew uneven. Given the difference in their heights, he could rest his cheek on the top of her head and feel the silk of her hair. While the idea was enticing, he kept his gaze fixed on the exit to the lobby. There was no reason for the two men to pass this way, but it didn't hurt to remain vigilant.

Words from a Hank Williams song about a lonesome past and a cold, cold heart drifted softly over them from a lobby speaker.

Though he craved a clearer view of the lobby, Corbin held back. He couldn't risk revealing their location. Instead, he monitored his breathing, counting down from one hundred while keeping his senses sharp. When he reached zero, he patted Beth's arm.

A single set of footsteps sounded across the tiled lobby, moving toward them. To be safe, he maneuvered his body to block Beth, then placed his hand beneath his coat for easier access to his Glock, if necessary.

The sharp-eyed clerk appeared, his hands clasped before his waist. "You've missed your co-workers, ma'am."

"Oh, uh, okay." She glanced at Corbin, searching for direction. "Did they say anything?"

"They just left," the clerk said. "I'm afraid they were a little confused. They weren't certain if they were work colleagues or relatives. They mentioned one thing on the phone, and another in person. Thought you should know."

"Absolutely," Corbin said. "You did the right thing."

Beth moved from behind Corbin. "You're certain they're gone?"

"Absolutely certain, ma'am. Watched the car pull away myself."

Corbin lowered his hand from his gun holster. "You didn't happen to get the make and model of the car?"

The clerk handed over a slip of paper he'd been holding in his clasped hands. "I wrote down all the information. Including the license plate number."

Corbin accepted the folded note with a shake of his head. "How did you know?"

"Instinct." The clerk shrugged. "You do this job long enough, you notice things."

"Thank you." Corbin shook the man's hand. "You into computers?"

"Some."

Corbin named an obscure tracking program used to trace online purchases. "Ever worked with it?"

"Too clunky and unsophisticated." The clerk named a superior program. "It's more detailed."

Corbin retrieved a business card from his pocket and jotted down his work number on the back. "If you ever decide to get out of the hotel business, let me know."

The clerk glanced at the card, and his eyes widened. "Cyber, huh? I may just take you up on that offer."

"We're always looking for people with good instincts."

"Anything else I can do for you, sir?"

"How about a taxi?"

"Can do." The clerk grinned. "You'll be hearing from me."

"I hope so."

As they crossed the lobby, Beth caught his arm. "How did they find us?"

While that piece of the puzzle haunted him, at least they'd finally caught a break. "I don't know."

"Maybe they spotted us leaving the restaurant last night," she said. "It was late. Dark. Not many places open that time of night. Wouldn't be difficult to guess where we'd gone."

Corbin glanced at the paper in his hand. "The

police should have scared them off, but it's possible. Anything is possible."

Either way, he finally had some leverage. He suspected they had someone in law enforcement back in Chicago. Probably a low-level clerk who fed them information now and then for an envelope of cash. He didn't need to find the leak. Not yet. He had something different in mind.

"What now?" Beth asked.

"Thanks to our friend, we've finally got the advantage." He flashed the paper. "Now we're tracking *them*."

The dealership Corbin had discovered online didn't appear entirely reputable.

Beth wrinkled her nose. "Are you certain about this?"

The lot sat on a corner between a Mexican restaurant and an abandoned gas station. Thirty or so vehicles in various stages of rusty, dented disrepair were neatly parked in diagonal slots. Most of them featured enormous balloons attached to the hoods, and several sported signs declaring the slogans: *Runs Great! Low Miles! Automatic Transmission!*

Corbin tented his hand and peered through a windshield. "I wanted someone who doesn't mind dealing in cash, and who doesn't feel the need to ask a lot of probing questions."

"Someone who advertises an automatic transmission?" Beth tugged on a balloon string. She pictured Sam Cross's smiling face, his son in his arms, and her smile faded. "They must be using the advertising signs from the eighties."

"I guess there was nothing else good to say."

"Now I'm worried." She let go of the string, and the balloon bobbed back into place. "That was nice what you did, for the clerk back there."

The hotel clerk's quick thinking had saved them a lot of time and trouble. Corbin's superior had run the car plates through the system. The security camera from the train station and the parking garage had revealed the same sedan.

Same plates. Same car. Same men.

The police had found the car almost immediately, though not the two men. They were on alert, but confident they'd be captured soon. Discovering the abandoned car had narrowed the search parameters. Either way, the loss of the car was bound to slow down the men. With the threat mitigated, they'd decided to purchase transportation. Corbin had chosen to keep their names off the radar. While she appreciated his caution, all the extra safeguards felt redundant.

"Nothing nice about it," Corbin said. He felt beneath the fender of the nearest car and retracted his hand. Rust flakes coated his fingertips. "The kid has good instincts. He was reading a spy novel while I was doing the crossword puzzle this morning. Figured he was wasted in the hotel business."

"It's freezing." Beth blew a puff of warm air into her cupped hands. "I should have waited for the California Zephyr and gone south."

"We'll buy you a new coat as soon as I finish here." He crouched and touched the dented fender of a *Runs Great!* Ford Eclipse. "Why'd you change your mind about going south in the first place?"

"The parking garage. After those men found me, I decided to change course."

He stood and dusted his hands. "Thought it was me."

"That, too."

Corbin's expression grew intense. He was studying her, as though trying to divine her thoughts. He needn't have bothered. Her thoughts were simple. She wanted this over. She wanted to go back to work at another company where nobody remembered her name.

Her heart sank. No. That wasn't true, either. She was tired of being anonymous. She wanted to feel as though she was a part of something bigger. While she enjoyed her work, moving from company to company had left her feeling empty. If only Timothy was here. He'd have some words or wisdom or some excellent advice. He'd known everything there was to know about the business of forensic accounting.

What she really wanted was to feel as though something she did made a difference to the greater good. That her work mattered.

Shivering, she blew another puff of air into her hands. "I'm buying a pair of gloves, too."

Corbin slipped out of his jacket and wrapped the material around her shoulders.

The lingering heat from his body immediately cocooned her in comforting warmth.

She attempted to shrug away. "I can't."

"I insist."

Too cold to argue, she merely nodded. If he didn't mind freezing, she didn't mind sharing his coat. She inhaled, and his comforting masculine scent filled her senses.

While she hopped from foot to foot to keep warm, he wove through the parked cars, his breath blowing clouds into the chill morning air. Though his bandage showed through the tear in his sleeve, the stains were gone. She pictured him rinsing out his shirt in the cramped hotel sink, and her stomach did an odd little flip.

The time and temperature scrolled past on the bank display across the street. "I thought this dealership was supposed to open at eight?"

"Let's give them another fifteen minutes."

Though the cars might not be in very good repair, someone cared enough to attach balloons and slogans. Five minutes passed before a tall, thin man wearing a tight, shiny suit appeared.

He caught sight of them and started. "What a lovely beginning to the day." He clapped his hands together and threaded his fingers. "I'm Frank. What can I do for you, folks?"

Corbin gestured toward the third car in the line nearest to him. "I'd like to look at that one."

"Let me get the keys."

After a quick test drive and inspection, Corbin offered a clipped, "We'll take it."

The 1994 Honda Prelude had a rusted fender, nearly two-hundred-thousand miles on the speedometer and a five-speed transmission. The gray interior matched the gray exterior, and the upholstery smelled slightly stale with an overlay of linen air freshener.

Beth whispered near his ear. "Can we afford that?"

"It's less than two tickets to Brussels."

"What does that mean?"

"Means I'll be reimbursed for what I withdrew from the ATM this morning."

"All right," the dealer said, naming a price. "You're getting a great deal."

Corbin shook his head. "That's not what your advertisement said."

"Well, that was before. Turns out, I got another buyer on the line for that price." The dealer splayed his hands. "But I like you. So if you want to pay a little extra, I'm willing to let it go to you. That's a good car. Solid. It's still a fair price."

Corbin braced his legs apart and crossed his arms. Beth cast an uneasy glance between the two men. They'd discussed their financial situation on the way over. They were sticking to cash as much as possible to avoid leaving a cyber trail. They didn't have enough for sticker price, but the amount Corbin had offered seemed reasonable, given the car's condition.

They also didn't have a lot of time to waste.

"Let the other guy have the car." Thinking quickly, Beth threaded her hand through the crook of Corbin's elbow and batted her eyelashes. "I don't like it, anyway, honey. It's too boring." She rubbed her hand up his arm, careful to glide over the bandaged area. "I liked the red one from the other dealership better. It's cute. And red."

Though she'd done plenty of public speaking in her career, the idea of pretending to be someone else had never held much appeal. Wearing Corbin's suit jacket, her freezing toes becoming tiny blocks of ice and the tip of her nose going numb, she warmed right up to the new role.

Corbin startled before a hint of a grin appeared. He wrapped his arm around her waist and stared into her eyes. "You know I can't deny you anything, Snickerdoodle. If you want the red car, we'll get the red car."

He was playing along, which helped, but she was really going to have to sell the ruse for this to work. Assuming a flirtatious smile, she walked her fingers across Corbin's chest. "You know red is my favorite color, darling."

Beth capped the declaration with a slight pout.

Corbin caught her fingers and pressed them against his lips. "How could I forget, sugar?"

The dealer was watching them with a deepening frown, the heel of his shiny shoe tapping, as though trying to decide if they were sincere or not. Beth gauged his response. Might as well lay it on a bit thicker. Not like they had anything to lose. She was freezing, and the sooner they bought a car, the sooner they could be on their way.

Nothing to be embarrassed about. After all, this wasn't Beth Greenwood behaving in such a ridiculous fashion, this was her alter ego.

Holding Corbin's arm for balance, she rose on her tiptoes to plant a kiss on his cheek. Except he turned. She hadn't been expecting him to turn. Their lips met, and her eyes flew open. A flock of butterflies took flight in her stomach. The kiss was quick.

The next instant he set her away from him. He stared at her, his expression one of brooding intensity, as though he was puzzling out a riddle.

Her hand remained pressed against his chest, against the rapid beating of his heart. The rhythm matched her own.

"Wait." The dealer held up his hands. "You're killing me, but I'll take the hit. Let me get the paperwork."

Beth stifled a gasp. Oh, dear. She'd gotten a bit lost in the role.

"Nah." Corbin tightened the arm holding her waist and backed them away. "The lady likes red. Could you deny her anything?"

He gazed at her again, the mask firmly back in place. With a light, flirtatious smile on his lips and amusement shimmering in his blue eyes, he winked.

"No. I mean, uh, yes," the dealer stuttered. "I have a red Pontiac Vibe."

He gestured vaguely in the direction of a car with a bobbing yellow balloon and an *Automatic Transmission!* sign.

"I don't think so," Corbin guided her toward the street. "Not even the color red can make a Vibe cool."

"Um." The dealer snapped his fingers. "How about I knock something off the price of the Honda? You know, to make up for the color."

She held her breath for Corbin's reply. They didn't exactly have the upper hand. She widened her eyes at Corbin, willing him to relent.

"I don't know." Corbin shook his head. "What do you think, Snickerdoodle?"

"Hmm." To put some space between them, she strolled to the car and peered in the window, then made a show of slowly circling around the front. "The Honda does have a cup holder armrest."

"That's mighty compelling." Corbin splayed his arms. "It's up to you, darling."

He winked again. He was giving her a signal. She sensed he was willing her to capitulate. Though no words were spoken between them, she'd become attuned to his moods. To his facial expressions. Never before had she been this instantly in sync with someone else. The feeling was heady. As though there was an invisible connection between them.

While her brain knew they were only playacting, her pulse thrummed. "Then let's buy the Honda."

"Absolutely, ma'am." The dealer grinned and hightailed it to the office before they changed their minds. He paused on the threshold. "I'll even throw in a balloon with the deal. Let me just get the paperwork started. I'll put on a pot of coffee, too."

Once he was out of earshot, Beth gave Corbin the side eye. "Snickerdoodle?"

"It was either that or Pop-Tart."

"You're right." She laughed. "I much prefer Snickerdoodle."

"At least we got a balloon out of the deal." Her expression fell, and Corbin grasped her hands. "What's wrong?"

"Every time I see a balloon, I think of Sam's son holding that balloon in the picture."

She'd been playacting. Enjoying herself when others were in mourning. Sam's family was devastated. They'd be calling his son at UCLA to break the news. There'd be tears. Policemen. Confusion. A family had been destroyed, and here she was, behaving as though nothing had changed.

Everything had changed. She could never go back to the person she was before this all started.

"I'm going to find out who killed Sam." Corbin gave her fingers a gentle squeeze. "Someone will pay. I promise you that."

"I know you will."

She didn't doubt his word. That wasn't the problem. She questioned her responsibility in Sam's death. If she'd asked for help earlier, would he still be alive? In her quest to save herself, had she caused the death of another?

"No," Corbin's voice interrupted her troubled thoughts. "Don't think like that."

"You don't know what I'm thinking."

"Even if you'd gone to the FBI immediately, there was nothing linking Sam to the money laundering. He'd have been vulnerable even if you had come to me sooner."

Astonished, she stared at him from beneath her eyelashes. "Maybe you do know what I'm thinking."

"Once the FBI tracks the information you discovered at Quetech, we'll find the people who killed Sam. No matter what happens, his death had nothing to do with the choices you made. For all we know, he interrupted a burglar."

"You don't really believe that, do you?"

The eyes behind his glasses grew hooded. "No."

"Me, neither."

He might have said something more, but the dealer returned, a sheaf of papers clutched in his hand. She remained silent, caught in her troubled thoughts, while Corbin signed for the car.

No matter what Corbin said, she'd never know whether or not her choices had set off the chain of events that had led to Sam's murder.

Whatever happened, she was done running. She was done hiding. No one else was going to be hurt because of the choices she'd made. Least of all Corbin. She'd started this process alone, and that's how she'd end things.

Her stomach pitched. Even if that meant running again.

EIGHT

An hour later, Corbin was driving the slightly musty-smelling Honda through the light weekend traffic. They'd stopped to buy a couple of burner phones and memorized each other's numbers.

Corbin glanced at a sign visible from the interstate. "Let's pull over and get some new clothes. I don't feel like washing these out in the sink again tonight."

"Agreed," Beth said immediately.

He drummed his finger on the steering wheel and considered his apology. The show of acting at the car dealership had gotten a little too personal. He couldn't read Beth's thoughts well enough to guess if she was angry, embarrassed, or scared of him—and he wasn't quite certain how to put her at ease.

"Hey, um," he began, "about what happened back there—"

"I am so sorry," she rushed ahead over his words. "That was all my fault. I only meant to kiss your cheek. I figured if that guy looked too close, he'd realize we didn't belong together."

Of all the things he'd expected her to say, that hadn't topped his list. "Why not?"

"Why not what?"

He thought they were just fine together. "Why don't we belong together?"

"Well, uh, you know. People in relationships tend to match each other. You know, they wear similar styles of clothing. You were dressed in work clothes. Good quality. I had on jeans and a hoodie. Even if they don't realize it, most people take note of those things on some level. I could tell he was suspicious of us."

That made sense. No reason to get his back up. "You have good instincts."

"That's why I was exaggerating the role. I figured if he was uncomfortable with our public affection, he'd be less likely to notice we didn't belong together."

"Your plan worked." Corbin had certainly been distracted. "We got a good price on the car."

"I'm sorry, though, about, well, you know. I hope I didn't make you too uncomfortable."

The heater in the Honda really worked well. He turned down the temperature. "Not uncomfortable. Don't worry. I, uh, meant to apologize, as well. I was, uh, trying to cover my surprise and may have reacted with a little too much enthusiasm."

The enthusiasm had less to do with his surprise, and more to do with his emotions taking over his good sense. Something that seemed to be happening far too often these days.

"Then we're good?" she asked with an overly chipper grin.

He'd been so uncomfortable with his part in the conversation, he hadn't realized she was suffering from her own embarrassment. "We're good. No worries."

To his immense relief, navigating the busy parking lot gave him a much-needed distraction. The large discount store featured clothing and home goods on one side, and groceries on the other. They could get everything they needed in one place.

Inside, he paused before the men's clothing section and stared at the rack. A sudden exhaustion overwhelmed him. He loathed shopping. All he needed was a quick change of clothing, but even that seemed troublesome. He rubbed his temple.

Beth tilted her head. "What?"

"I don't like shopping." He liked it even less when he considered that Beth was staring at him. "That's the nice thing about being in the military. The uniforms. You don't have to decide what to wear."

"Do you mean to tell me that the man who took

a bullet yesterday is balking at the thought of picking out clothes?"

"That's exactly what I'm telling you." He lifted a shirt from the rack and set it back down again. "Maybe I'll look at jeans first." He turned toward the display and groaned. "When I was a kid, there were three choices of jeans. They didn't figure men needed any more than three choices. What changed? Why did it change?"

Beth covered her eyes and shook her head. "All right, tough guy, I'll tell you what—why don't you let me pick out a few things for you?"

"All right." A vague, annoying sense of unease skittered through him. He didn't know if that was better or worse than picking things out for himself. Probably worse. He'd never been particularly fond of his mom's choice of clothing, and she was the last person who'd ever bought him anything to wear. "But nothing too colorful. Or tight, or—"

Beth held up a hand. "Just relax. We'll get through this together." She reached for a neon-orange hoodie. "Too much?"

"Yes!"

"I'm joking. Did your mom force you to wear Toughskins when you were growing up?"

The tips of his ears heated. "Something like that."

She'd made him and Evan wear matching outfits on Christmas Eve until they'd gotten old enough to rebel.

"All right," Beth said. "I'm not forcing you to buy anything. You have final approval on whatever you want to wear."

Well, now he just felt like an even bigger idiot. "Fine. You win. Let's just get this over as quickly as possible."

Forty-five minutes later, Corbin had to admit she had good taste. After ringing up their purchases, they ducked into separate bathrooms and changed. He'd agreed to purchase a navy-blue button-down shirt, a pair of jeans and a dark brown canvas coat.

Dumping his torn shirt in the trash felt good. As though he was letting go of the previous day. Of his previous mistakes. He was relatively certain there was no way they were being tracked, but he still wasn't letting down his guard.

Beth stepped out of the bathroom and caught sight of him. "Not bad. I might be in the wrong business."

Two men passed through the front door. They were about the same height and build of the men who'd been following them. Beth snatched his hand.

"Not them," he said immediately, sensing her distress.

As the two men neared, it was clear they were father and son.

"I owe you an apology for what I said last night." She retracted her hand. "I'm starting to understand how you feel. Everything seems sinister these days. I'm looking at everyone with new eyes. Your job must really get to you."

"Some days are more difficult than the others. We should get going."

Her words had haunted him the previous evening. *What must it be like to see everyone as a threat?* It was far easier than dying, that was for certain.

It was one of those rare autumn days when the air was frigid cold, but the sun painfully bright. The blast of cold air hit them like a wall. Beth tugged her new gloves over her wrists and yanked the coat tighter around her middle.

As they reached the car, he swung open the door. "Appreciating the new gear?"

"Most definitely."

He navigated the car back on to the interstate and headed north. The frosty air reminded him of being a kid in Wisconsin. Of playing in the snow until his fingers and toes ached. Despite the cooler temperatures, the area had yet to experience a snowfall, leaving the landscape in dull shades of brown and rust. The trees were nothing but bare skeleton branches etched against the horizon.

Corbin viewed a map on his new phone and navigated the traffic.

"You said you worked a case here?" Beth asked. "You seem to know your way around."

"Last year." They'd had a report of suspicious activity from a bank teller who worked in the suburbs. It hadn't taken long to figure out the clerk had been too enthusiastic in his profiling. "Spent about six weeks living downtown. Middle of the winter. Thought I was going to be miserable, but I discovered cross-country skiing. Ever tried?"

"Nope."

He shrugged. "I always try something new when I visit a city. Helps alleviate the boredom. What do you do?"

"Um. I jog. Sometimes I visit a museum or something. I read a lot. There aren't many places a person can visit alone without standing out."

He pictured her hovering near the break room as everyone else sang "Happy Birthday." He hadn't considered how her job always kept her on the outside looking in. She was always the new employee, never staying long enough to be truly included. Though he'd done plenty of undercover work, he had a home base. Someplace that kept him centered. What did Beth have? He didn't suppose most people warmed to a forensic accountant right away.

"That must get lonely," he said.

"Not really." She kept her gaze fixed on the passing scenery. "I'm used to being alone."

"You're an only child, right?" He knew a few facts about her. Age. Address. Family background. But he didn't know anything about her personally. "I suppose that makes a difference."

What else had he learned along the way? She always recycled. She never took the elevator—even when she was wearing heels—and she had a weakness for expensive chocolate. Every Friday for the past two weeks, she'd visited the neighboring department store during her lunch hour, returning with a small, foil-wrapped box of truffles. Four truffles that lasted through the following week.

She fiddled with the zipper on her new coat. "I think it depends more on your personality than whether or not you're an only child. I'm an introvert. I'm not much for crowds. Or, um, new people. What about you? Do you have brothers and sisters?"

For a moment he hesitated. This was a mistake. While he was supposed to be getting to know her, he should be protecting himself. Yet he didn't see the harm in sharing rudimentary information. He'd asked her a personal question, after all. She had every right to inquire about him, as well.

"I had an older brother," he said. "Evan was killed in Afghanistan a few years ago."

"That's when you got the tattoo?" her voice was hushed.

"Yep."

Evan had died forty-three months ago this week, to be exact. The pain was still there. It had never completely dulled. He could forget, for a while. The passage of time had whittled away the sharpest edges.

There were times when he could behave as though everything was normal. But there were other times, the oddest times, when a memory brought his brother to the forefront of his mind, and he felt as though the loss was yesterday.

Lately he couldn't help but wonder about the future. When did it get easier? When would he be able to speak of Evan's death without feeling as though the loss was three hours ago instead of nearly four years before?

"I'm sorry," Beth said quietly. "Losing your only brother. That must have been devastating."

"Yeah."

Devastating was as good a word as any. He'd felt ripped apart, as though he'd lost of a vital piece of himself, of his memories. He and his brother had a shared history, and sometimes it felt as though that history had disintegrated with Evan's death.

He glanced over to find Beth staring at him. He quickly shifted his attention back to the road.

"What was he like?" she asked.

The question took him by surprise. Most people

changed the subject. Most people feared walking into an emotional minefield.

Unaccustomed to follow-up questions, he struggled to form his thoughts. "Evan was the outgoing kid in the family. Impulsive. Reckless. He mellowed as he got older. After he joined the military."

"Did you follow in his footsteps? Is that why you joined the army?"

It all seemed like a lifetime ago. He hadn't thought about his decision in years. "Sort of. I always knew I wanted to serve. My family didn't have a lot of money growing up. Figured joining the military was the only way I was going to pay for my education. Evan was two years older, but he didn't join right away. He did some traveling after graduation. He didn't really have a direction. He was good at everything, and everything came easy to him. Then one day I got a call. He was in boot camp."

"Just like that?" She whistled softly. "Didn't he tell anyone? Not even your parents?"

"Nope. Said he talked to a recruiter. Signed the papers the next day. Just made up his mind, I guess. Same thing when he got married. Called the family from Hawaii."

"Wow. That's crazy. I can't imagine making a life-changing decision like that on the spur of the moment. I once bought a sofa and agonized over the decision for a month."

Corbin chuckled. "That was Evan. Once he got something into his head, there was no stopping him. So I guess you could say I followed in his footsteps, because he went through boot camp first. I was still in school when he did his first tour of duty."

"What was your plan when you enlisted?"

He shook his head. "You don't get to plan when you're in the military. The army makes a plan for you, and that's how it's done."

"Can you tell me about your job?" She flashed a grin. "Or will you have to kill me?"

"I can tell you some." He caught sight of his exit and signaled a lane change. "I worked in crypto. Had a top-secret security clearance. Spent most of my time stateside working in underground bunkers or in buildings without windows. After Evan died, I requested a transfer. Did my last year in Afghanistan. I liked the change of scenery."

This was delving into increasingly personal areas, but he didn't see the harm. This was his history. Nothing anyone couldn't find out with an internet search.

"But you didn't reenlist, even though you liked the scenery?" Her voice lifted at the end of the sentence in question.

"Nope. I didn't reup." He hardly even remembered making the decision. He didn't recall much from that time. Everything had turned into a blur.

"Why not?"

"Well—"

"Never mind." She touched his sleeve. "You don't have to answer if that's too personal."

"Nah. I'm just not sure I have an answer."

Oddly, it felt good talking about Evan. It felt good speaking honestly. Though he and his parents spoke plenty about Evan, there was always an edge in their conversation. They only told the happy stories. They only shared the fond memories. As though bringing up anything negative denigrated his brother's memory. Not that anything could denigrate Evan's memory with his parents.

Evan had been full of life. When he'd gotten into trouble growing up, there was usually a wink and a nod with his punishment. For his senior prank, he'd stolen all the For Sale signs out of the neighborhood yards and planted them in the schoolyard. He'd been forced to return the signs. But he'd returned them with such a cheerful sense of fun that most of the homeowners had been amused instead of angry. It had been impossible not to like Evan, which had made his death all the more shattering.

"I was watching my family fall apart," Corbin said. The silence between them in the car was companionable, and he found he wanted to answer. "They didn't take Evan's death well. My mom was worried. Calling me every day. Crying. She didn't even know I was working covert ops. She thought I was still sitting behind a desk. My dad was calling because my mom was upset. Then one day my nephew sent a letter. Asked if I was gonna die, too. I just couldn't do it to them anymore. I didn't love the job like I had in the beginning. I wanted to decide where I was going to live without someone handing me orders. The timing just seemed right. My commanding officer had retired a year before. He took a job stateside. Got me an interview. Here we are."

He'd been living in a fog following Evan's death. He'd worked obsessively, but he was wading into a bottomless pit. There was so much evil in the world. So much suffering. The despair was seeping into his bones and turning him cynical. He'd had to get out while there was still some humanity left in him. He'd had to get out while he still believed there was good in people.

He could have done his twenty years and pulled a full retirement; he was good at his job, and there was always another terrorist cell to track—but he hadn't.

What is it like, seeing everyone as a threat?

It was lonely. Like always being the outsider.

Beth adjusted her seat and leaned against the headrest. "That was an incredibly kind thing to do."

He grunted. "Not really. It was a way of covering up the fact that I was afraid. I was afraid I was going to make a mistake and get someone killed. Evan trusted the wrong person, and that mistake cost him his life."

Corbin had quit for reasons that had nothing to do with kindness. He was afraid he was going to make a decision that got an innocent killed.

He'd quit because he was a coward.

NINE

Beth caught something in Corbin's expression, in his voice, something that indicated a deeper meaning behind his words.

"There's nothing wrong with being afraid." She adjusted her seat belt and turned toward him. "My dad was a Chicago policeman. He was a good cop. They put him in charge of training the younger recruits. He always said that he never trusted a recruit who wasn't a little afraid. They were too reckless. They were too impulsive. He always thought a little fear kept a man alive."

"Your dad sounds like a good man," Corbin said.

"He was." A wave of melancholy crashed over her. "I miss him." She pressed her hand against the chilly window, and the glass fogged around her fingertips. "Were your brother's killers brought to justice?"

She'd always considered herself a loner, but lately she was starting to wonder if she understood her own nature. She was restless. Unsatisfied. Despite being an introvert, she craved a connection. She'd lost the two people in life who mattered most to her, and there was an empty space in her heart.

"His killers were caught." Corbin imbued the sentence with a wealth of meaning. "Evan had gotten a tip that a high-value target was holed up in a local village. His unit infiltrated with a small detail, afraid of alarming the man. The tip was a setup. His unit was ambushed."

Beth gasped. "I'm so sorry."

"It's a waste. All that suffering for one bad piece of intel."

One mistake. Life was both incredibly durable and incredibly fragile. They were all one mistake away from death at any given moment. One moment of distracted driving. One slip and fall. Time was a precious, valuable commodity, and one that she often took for granted.

Was she doing good with the time she had? Was she honoring those whose time had been cut short? Was she honoring God with her life? She hadn't let himself slow down long enough to answer those questions.

He glanced at his phone and then at a street sign. "This is our exit."

After they turned off the interstate, traffic grew heavier. They left the city behind and entered the suburbs. Tidy houses lined the tree-lined streets. Hedges, dormant for the winter, were neatly trimmed. Cheerful painted signs pointed the way toward the Harvest Festival. As they neared the last turnoff, a line of cars stretched toward the parking lot.

Beth tapped her foot on the floor and glanced behind them. "Popular place. Any updates on our two stalkers?"

"No." He glanced at his phone again. "I thought we'd hear something by now. In an abundance of caution, I alerted local security. Can't hurt to have more eyes on the situation. Orders are not to approach, merely inform. I want information not an incident."

She hoped the news of the men's arrests came soon. All they had to do was make it to Tuesday morning. On Tuesday morning, everyone would know the truth. They'd have the evidence. They'd have the proof. There'd be no reason to doubt her anymore.

As Corbin followed the signs to the festival, the dubious suspension on the Honda bumped over the gravel road. A couple hundred cars filled the parking lot. Good cover to get lost in the crowd. Despite the heavy traffic, they managed to find a parking spot near the front entrance.

Corbin dialed his phone and spoke for a few

minutes before hanging up. "The plates were stolen. No good leads. Professionals."

"They also got their car impounded. That should slow them down."

He put the car in gear and rested his hands on the steering wheel. "This parking spot is good for a quick exit. Let's hope we don't need it."

"You don't actually believe they could still be tracking us?" Beth snorted softly. "They don't even have a car now. That must give us some leeway. You've alerted the security at the festival. You've alerted the local police."

"I let down my guard once," he said. "I'm not making the same mistake twice."

She swiveled in her seat. "Then, what now?"

"We'll make a few rounds inside the event, then circle back to the car. On the off chance they've followed us this far, the misdirection should ditch them."

"I understand being cautious, but don't see how they can be tracking us." She made a sound of frustration, her hands strangling the air. "We've dumped everything." Raising her foot, she gestured. "I even have on new socks. *New socks.* We're driving a car that we bought this morning. How in the world can they be tracking us?"

"I don't know," he said, appearing equally frustrated. "But something is tipping them off. Minneapolis is a big city, and they wound up at our hotel."

"Maybe they saw us leaving the restaurant last night. You said it yourself. There aren't many places open at that time of night. All they had to do was stake out the bars that were within walking distance of the train station. It wouldn't be impossible."

"This is my job. This is what I do for a living. All the proof tells me that we've ditched them. But I don't know who else is out there. I don't know what we're dealing with. This place is filled with people, and there's plenty of security. No one is going to try anything here. I'd feel better if we went with the original plan, even if it's just an exercise in futility."

She tapped her fingers on the dash. "If you're this worried, why don't you simply turn me over to the FBI?"

"At the risk of being blunt, they don't want you. Without the evidence, you have nothing to offer. Once that email arrives, we'll be in a position to negotiate."

"Then why don't you turn me over to the police?" she asked quietly.

"Because I'm afraid that's exactly what these men want," Corbin said. "They want to discredit you. They want to tear your world apart. I believe they're laying the groundwork to frame you for embezzlement and maybe even murder. Once you're in police custody, we lose bargaining power. We'll be mired in the false charges for weeks before we can sort through the mess."

"But none of that should matter to you. You'll have the email. You'll have the proof. What difference does it make if I'm in a jail somewhere?"

"You matter." He took her hands in his warm clasp. "I believe you're trying to do the right thing. I don't want you to be hurt any more than necessary."

Unexpected tears burned behind her eyes. "All right. I trust you. We'll play it safe."

He was doing this for her. He'd put his trust in her. Not right away, and not easily, but he'd turned a corner. She wasn't going to question his methods. He was the one person who believed in her.

She glanced around. "What are we waiting for?"

"I want to wait a few minutes, watch the traffic, just to be sure."

She reached for the door handle. "Then you won't mind if I take advantage of the facilities. All that coffee I drank this morning is starting to catch up with me."

She spotted a public restroom sign near the front entrance and jerked her thumb in the general direction. He'd be able to see her entering and exiting, which should make him feel better.

"Sure thing," he said, his tone distracted.

She paused for a moment, her hand on the

door. Her thoughts circled back to the train station. Maybe someone in Corbin's office had tipped them off. Maybe the transmitter had been in her phone. For all they knew, the two men had seen them leaving the restaurant. It was dark. They'd been exhausted.

There was one thing she knew for certain: there was no possible way they were still being tracked.

Beth hopped out of the car and jogged off, her ponytail bobbing along with her easy stride. Corbin watched for a moment before looking away. He had to keep watch over her for the sake of the investigation—nothing else. He certainly shouldn't be noticing that she had the easy, rolling gait of someone accustomed to jogging.

She'd left her backpack on the seat, and the price tag still dangled from the zipper.

He reached for the bag, and a chill snaked down his spine. He glanced at the small building Beth had disappeared into, and back at the bag. He'd trusted her to rid herself of her belongings, but she wasn't a professional. She might have missed something.

He tamped down his twinge of guilt. This was part of his job.

Without giving himself time to regret his actions, he dumped the contents of her bag on to the seat. The new clothing they'd purchased this morning was quickly tossed aside. He caught sight of her money pouch and unzipped the top. Carefully thumbing through each of the bills, he searched the contents. Nothing.

He shook the backpack again, and something rattled. A second pocket. He unzipped the compartment and several makeup items tumbled free along with a small, framed picture.

She'd said she'd dumped everything. Not the picture. He recognized the frame from her desk at Quetech. There was a scratch marring the wood. Same picture. Same frame.

Her dad had been a cop. He'd understand. "Sorry, sir," Corbin mumbled to the picture. "But I have to know."

He cracked open the picture frame and searched the back, then sagged against the seat. Nothing.

A shadow darkened the car window, and he glanced up. A young couple pushing a stroller passed by. He didn't have much time. As he replaced Beth's belongings into the backpack, her makeup compact slipped off the seat and hit the floor. The top burst open releasing a cosmetic sponge.

Stretching across the gearshift, he reached for the plastic case. As he placed the round makeup sponge back into the tray, something caught his eye.

He held the plastic to the light. A raised metallic

square had been attached to the hollow bottom of the compact where the makeup sponge was stored.

His pulse jerked. He knew how the two men discovered the hotel.

They'd been tracked, all right.

Beth sensed something was wrong the minute she resumed her seat in the car. "What is it?"

The crease in Corbin's brow folded in on itself. "You got rid of everything, right?"

"Yes," she insisted.

"What about this?" He displayed her father's picture. "And this?" He held her compact in the other hand.

"You went through my bag!" A flush spread across her face. "What gives you the right to go through my belongings?"

"This." He yanked his badge from his pocket. "This is my job, Beth. Or had you forgotten that?"

Her cheeks burned. "I searched every inch of that picture and frame. There's nothing there. You saw yourself. I couldn't leave it behind. It's the only thing I have of h-him." Her voice caught on the last word.

"But what about this?"

He displayed her makeup compact once more.

"You're being ridiculous. That's just makeup. I bought it on Friday. A little retail therapy." She was babbling now, but the way he was looking at her had the blood rushing through her veins. "I went shopping at the department store next to Quetech. I didn't even take it out of the box until last night."

She adored the decadent feel of the packages. Not to mention it was free-gift time. Getting the free gift always made her feel better about the exorbitant amount of money she was spending.

Given Corbin's frowning countenance, he probably wasn't interested in hearing about her Friday afternoon adventures.

He flipped open the lid. "Look."

She squinted, and her stomach dropped. "Oh, no."

"Oh, yes." He indicated the raised circle attached to the plastic. "This is definitely a tracking device."

"But... I... I don't understand. I told you, I just took it out of the box this morning."

"When did you buy it?"

"On Friday, during lunch break. I always go shopping on Friday. For, you, know..."

"Chocolate."

The sense of betrayal sucked the breath from her lungs. "How could I forget? You've been spying on me."

She'd let down her guard. His easygoing manner had lured her into a false sense of trust. No matter what he'd said before, he didn't trust her.

In the end, she didn't mean anything to him. She was a means to an end. Nothing more.

"Don't turn everything into a conspiracy," he said easily. "I noticed you disappeared every Friday and returned with chocolate. You walked right past my office. We'd chat."

"Would you have talked to me otherwise?" She'd deliberately walked past his office because she enjoyed their chats. He was cute. He was nice. He made her pulse flutter. And everything he'd said to her while he was working at Quetech had been a lie. "Was any of what you said to me true just now?"

"Yes. Everything I said to you just now is true." He indicated the makeup compact. "Including the part where I discovered a tracking device in your backpack."

"They shot at me, too, you know."

"I know. That's why we're having this conversation in a parked car, and why I'm not hauling you into the local police department. You're telling me this was brand-new on Friday?"

"Yes." She narrowed her gaze. "That's why I didn't throw it away." And also because it was really expensive. But mostly because she didn't see how or when someone could have attached a tracking device. She still didn't. "That hasn't been out of my sight."

"Not even at work?"

"No. I keep my purse in a locked drawer." She recalled her last day. She'd been nervous. Too nervous to eat. She'd done some more shopping instead. The line had taken longer than she'd expected, and she'd barely returned in time for an afternoon meeting. She'd locked her purse in the drawer. The department store bag hadn't fit. She'd shoved it behind a row of folders. No one stole makeup, she'd figured. How did anyone know if the color matched? "That's wrong. I left the bag on my desk."

"All right. Let's think." He pinched the bridge of his nose. "When was the last time you used the compact?"

"Never. I haven't had a chance." She braced her hands against the dashboard. The full impact was sinking in, and her stomach lurched. "I never even considered there might have been something in the compact. It's been a crazy couple of days. I haven't exactly been primping in front of the mirror."

"I believe you. You don't need to justify anything."

Beth's heart leaped into her throat. "What?"

"This means whoever was tracking us was in the Quetech building. Not in the parking garage."

"Someone at Quetech did this? One of the other employees?"

"Most likely. Think about it, though. You said it

yourself on Friday. No one does anything in that building without leaving a cyber trail. We need to get access to the security cameras inside the building. If Homeland Security is already looking at the footage from the parking garage, we can get a warrant for the internal footage. If we can narrow down the time frame, we can make it easier on everybody."

Friday wasn't that long ago, but she felt as though she was looking back on a different person. "Sam did his presentation in the morning. I got back from lunch just before one o'clock. There was a staff meeting that lasted until two-fifteen."

"All right. That helps. And you didn't see anything unusual when you left?"

"No. And I was looking. I was paranoid. The building was clearing out. They'd let everyone off early for the holiday."

"All right. That narrows it down to a brief window. Anything helps."

Her head throbbed. Had she been reading Corbin all wrong? He wasn't blaming her. She'd fallen into the same trap she'd accused him of creating. "We can also rule out everyone who was in the meeting."

"Wait." He pivoted on his seat. "Was Sam in that staff meeting?"

"No." She whipped around. She'd been so distracted by her own problems, she hadn't paid much attention to anyone else. "He probably should have been. I never thought to ask. Janice was there, though. Matt was there. I remember because he came in late. A couple of other people from other departments. I didn't know them."

"That should make pinpointing the time of Sam's death easier." He studied the cosmetics case, holding it up to the light. "Now we have to think of something special to do with this little guy."

"Like get out of here," she said. "Fast. They might be sending another team to find us since the first one hasn't been doing such a great job."

"This isn't the movies. Putting a second team in place takes time. If they even have a second team." He brought up the map on his phone and expanded the picture. "They have to find another car since they've been compromised. I say we take this opportunity to feed them a little misinformation."

"How do we do that?"

"By sending this transmitter on a little a trip. C'mon. It's time for some mini donuts."

She stepped from the car, but her legs had gone weak. She took a few steps and sagged against the hood. Everything that had happened was her fault. The shoot-out at the train station. Everything. She'd been leading the two goons along every step of the way. Putting both her and Corbin in danger at every turn. She'd thought she'd been careful. Certain she'd thought of everything, but they'd been a step ahead of her the whole time. She'd had too much pride to see what was painfully obvious.

She wrapped her hands around her middle as though to hold herself together.

Corbin circled around the car. "Don't blame yourself. You didn't know. To be honest, I assumed they'd tracked your phone. If I'd been more vigilant last night, none of this would have happened."

She'd blamed him for believing the worst about her when she'd been guilty of her own sanctimony.

"You finally trusted me." He was giving her a moment to collect herself, and she appreciated his thoughtfulness. "I'm sorry. I just don't know what else to say."

"The important thing is that we know. We know how they were tracking us, which means we know they can't follow us anymore. That's a good outcome. The best."

"But you were shot." She gestured toward his arm. "They met us at the train station. That is not a good outcome."

He rolled his shoulder. "You didn't pull the trigger. We've discovered some very rotten people, and you're going to help me catch them. End of story."

"But…"

"No buts. We're at a festival. There are mini do-nuts. Nothing bad can happen at a place with mini donuts."

She offered him a watery smile. "Are you sure? Is it safe?"

"It's probably the safest place we can be right now. I'll request some extra patrols in the area. We'll ditch the GPS device, and be long gone by the time they get here. Security will be on the lookout. This is the best place to trap them."

She straightened, but her legs weren't steady, and she pitched forward. She caught a handful of his shirt to right herself, then swayed forward, drawn to him. He caught her around the shoulders and crushed her against his chest.

He was solid and safe, the warmth of his body soothing her frayed nerves. His faint breath stirred her hair, and his arm tightened around her, holding her steady. She hadn't felt truly safe since Timothy's death. She'd been so naive, thinking she could turn over the evidence and escape unscathed. Thinking that she didn't need any help.

For the past three years, since her dad's death, she'd been pushing all her feelings aside, as though she might visit them on a rainy day, but she was only putting off the inevitable. She hadn't slowed down long enough to think about how isolated she'd become. How lonely.

The unremitting threat of the situation had lowered her defenses, unlocking all those buried emotions. They were tumbling over her in waves. Loneliness. Sorrow. Fear.

Underneath everything there was a vague sense of dissatisfaction. She wanted something, but she didn't know what. She wanted something that was just out of reach.

Or maybe she simply wanted something she could never have.

"Everything is going to be fine, Beth," Corbin whispered against her hair. "You'll see. This is all going to be over soon."

His heart beat against her ear, strong and rhythmic, and in that moment, she didn't want their time together to be over. She wanted to stay here in the shelter of his embrace and feel safe. She wanted to feel connected to someone. If only for this moment.

She wasn't the same naive fool she'd been before. This was all going to be over, and she was never going to see him again.

Though she knew her feelings were heightened by the situation, she didn't care. She wrapped her arms around his waist and held him tight. She'd give herself this one moment.

She pressed her forehead against his chest. "I wish you were really the new financial consultant at Quetech Industries. I wish we'd gone to see Janice sing karaoke. I wish we could have had that coffee on Fifth street."

"Me, too."

"You don't have to say that. It's all right." Everything she felt for him was based on a lie. "I don't even know who you are. Not really."

He tucked two fingers beneath her chin and gently tilted her head. "You know everything you need to know about me." He was gazing at her with those ice-blue eyes, his expression tender. "You've been torturing me for the past two weeks, Beth Greenwood."

"I don't understand."

"I'm supposed to be impartial. Detached. I can't be. Not with you." He gently gripped her shoulders, setting her away from him. "And that's dangerous. For both of us. I have to keep you safe, and for that, I have to remain impartial. Alert. That sort of distraction could get us both killed. Do you understand?"

"Yes."

"We can't." He speared his fingers through his hair. "Anything that happens between us risks the job. Risks the case against Cayman Holdings and Quetech. After everything you've been through, I can't let that happen."

"It's all right," she said quietly. "I understand."

He searched her face, his gaze intense. "It's not personal—"

"I understand." She was part of an investigation. Any relationship was off-limits. What future did they have together, anyway? She was an accountant. She craved a sense of order in her life. A modicum of predictability. Routine. His life was anything but. "We're wasting time. I want that tracker far away."

"Agreed." He slid his hands into his pockets. "Now c'mon. We have to dump this tracker and try those mini donuts. In that order."

There was no use pining over the impossible. If she was lonely, then it was time she sought out a relationship. A healthy relationship with someone who shared her interests.

Her heart ached a bit. She wanted someone who wore glasses and looked a lot like a superhero from a comic book.

Maybe she'd even see about getting a job that kept her in town for more than a few weeks at a time. She was lonely because she'd chosen to conduct her life in a solitary manner. The time had come for a change.

She glanced at Corbin and firmed her resolve. He was keeping a distance between them. Holding part of himself back from her. He'd set the parameters of their relationship, and she owed it to him to respect those parameters. Considering the danger they were facing, her personal problems didn't amount to a hill of beans.

With that sobering thought, she and Corbin paid the entrance fee to the harvest festival and were presented with pumpkin stickers to wear on their coats.

She glanced at the smiling Jack-o'-lantern. "It's almost too bad Tweedledum and Tweedledumber aren't here. I want to see them wearing one of these stickers." She was still struggling with the realization that someone from her workplace had planted a tracking device on her possessions, and right under her nose. "How far can the device transmit?"

Concentrating on something solid helped focus her thoughts back to the problem at hand.

"It's a short-range transmitter with a lithium battery," Corbin said. "Like a watch battery, only smaller. The range is probably only a hundred miles. If they followed you to Union Station, all they had to do was wait for the signal to move in order to discover what train you'd taken. It's not that hard to tell where a train is going."

Corbin guided her through a maze of towering pumpkins. There were colorful scarecrows pointing the way to different attractions, along with several wooden cutouts. A laughing couple posed behind a pressboard cutout of a pumpkin carriage complete with gingham curtains on the windows.

"But how'd they know we'd get off in Minneapolis?" Beth asked.

"They probably didn't. They had to reach each stop ahead of us and wait. At least they don't know who I am. That works to our advantage. They don't know you've been in contact with Homeland Security."

A large sign cut in the shape of a hand pointed the way to the Moaning River. Nice touch for a fall-themed festival.

He squinted into the distance. "This way."

The festival was crowded for the weekend, and people jostled around them. An animatronic band in tattered Old West clothing played a jarring bluegrass tune from a wooden stage. The smell of kettle corn, roasted turkey legs and apple cider combined to form an odor that might have been an air freshener marked "fall festival."

Despite the events of the past two days, the festive mood of the crowd was contagious.

A dejected-looking preteen scuffed the dirt packed road. "I can't believe the corn maze isn't open yet."

His mother rolled her eyes. "They're behind schedule. We'll come back again another time."

"You always say stuff like that, but you never mean it," the teenager complained.

The mother's lips pursed. "I said we'll come back, and we'll come back."

"I didn't expect it to be this crowded," Corbin muttered beside her. "Who knew so many people liked pumpkins? Even if someone had followed us this far, they'd never find us." He paused before a small shack offering fresh mini donuts. "We didn't get to finish our breakfast this morning. We'll eat 'em while we walk. Won't slow us down."

"All right," she conceded with a shrug. "Since we're already here, we might as well."

The donuts turned out to be as wonderful as the waitress had predicted. They were crisp and sugary on the outside, and warm and soft on the inside. The worker served them a heaping pile in a square paper bowl.

"These are almost worth dying for," Beth sighed. "Almost."

They joined the tide of people moving in a general direction of Moaning River. Along the way they passed a pyramid of pumpkins, a pen containing goats, and a large barn-like building called the "pie hut."

Corbin polished off the last of the donuts, flipped over the square basket, and tapped the remaining sugar into a trash bin. Moaning River wound its way through the festival grounds, passing beneath a picturesque covered bridge.

He fished the makeup compact from his pocket. "We're going to set this a sail."

"Is there any chance of removing the tracking device first?" She gazed longingly at the expensive purchase. "I haven't even used that compact."

"It's been glued down. I'm afraid it's a lost cause."

"Fine," she grumbled.

That was the least of her worries, after all.

Corbin moved to the water's edge and crouched. He placed the compact in the donut-bowl-turned-boat and launched them both down the stream. Heavy fall rains had swollen the banks, and the makeshift boat danced merrily along with the current.

"That should throw them off the trail for a little while." Corbin stuffed his hands back in his pockets and gestured with his bent elbow. "Come along. We'll get some caramel apples for the road."

She kept her gaze averted. "What happens next?"

"Everything depends on what information you were able to retrieve from the Quetech computers. Until your email arrives, we're in a holding pattern."

"What do we do while we're waiting?"

"We'll drive at least as far as Chicago tonight. Farther if I can stay awake."

"Chicago?" She gaped. "You probably only slept four or five hours last night. And your arm.

You were shot. Shouldn't we stay here another night? Shouldn't we rest or something?"

"I don't need much sleep. Besides, Chicago is just the first stop. If nothing has changed by then, we'll keep going to Virginia. It's going to be a grueling trip. Homeland Security will need to trace the evidence you discovered."

"What's this all about, anyway?" She paused beside a rabbit pen containing a row of miniature wooden buildings marked Bunnyville. "What do you think the terrorist cell is targeting?"

"Doesn't matter. We'll stop them before they can execute the plan. They've been getting money to operate. We'll follow the money. Oldest trick in the book."

Though the two goons were still out there, discovering the tracking device had released a huge pressure. Between that and knowing the two men had been forced to ditch their car, both of them felt the change. As though a great weight had been lifted. They walked in companionable silence back through the festival grounds. There were loads of families out for the day, and the mood was infectious.

While Corbin laughed at a puppet, his eyes were constantly scanning the crowd. He remained vigilant and watchful.

She turned and collided with a woman holding

a cup of cider. The scalding liquid splashed over her coat. Beth shrieked and held the soaked material away from her skin.

"I'm so sorry!" the woman dabbed at the spot with a ridiculously small napkin.

"Don't worry." Beth fanned the material. "It was my fault."

The woman murmured more apologies before scurrying off.

"You all right?" Corbin asked.

"I'll smell great for the ride," she offered wryly. "I need to dry off."

"There's a bathroom near the exit."

The scalding liquid quickly cooled, and she was shivering by the time they reached the low building. She ducked into the bathroom and rinsed off the apple cider as best she could, then held her coat under the hand drier. The powerful burst of air sent the material rippling. Ten minutes later, she emerged into the chill, overcast afternoon once more. The coat was stained, but mostly dry.

She took a step, and someone snatched her arm.

The round barrel of a gun pressed into her side. Blood roared in her ears. She jerked away, but the hand wrapped around her upper arm tightened like a steel vice.

"Move," the fraudulent agent from the train station spoke, his voice low. "Don't even think about giving me any trouble. If I have to shoot, the bullet is liable to go right through you and hit some poor, innocent bystander. You wouldn't that now, would you?"

TEN

Corbin caught sight of Van and lunged.

A woman pushing a stroller passed in front of him. He jerked. His knee twisted, and he hopped awkwardly to one side, managing to avoid a collision at the last second. The baby in the stroller grinned at his antics. The mother glared. The delay cost him.

By the time Corbin righted himself, Van had his hand pressed against Beth's side. Holding a gun, no doubt. A shock of wild anguish roared through Corbin. He'd underestimated their growing desperation. Where were the extra patrols? The security checks at the gate? Someone had failed in their responsibility, and Beth was paying the price.

Corbin ducked behind a rowdy crowd of teenagers. At least he hadn't blown his cover. Van was focused on navigating the crowd, not looking around for Beth's "boyfriend." No second man was visible, either. Raynor and Van must have separated to search the festival.

He wrestled his wayward emotions and rapidly calculated his options. Van couldn't do anything now. Not with this many witnesses. Which bought Corbin some time. Currently, his only choice was to watch and wait. Though frustrated, he kept his pace measured.

They were near an exit, but Van was urging Beth in the opposite direction. Corbin followed them, keeping close watch, and icy focus took hold of him. Assess. Execute. They weren't leaving the fairgrounds with Beth.

Thankfully, the crowd of rowdy teenagers co-operated. As long as they were heading in the same direction, he had cover.

Beth's head swung from side to side, looking for him, no doubt, and his stomach plummeted. There was no way to signal her. Not without giving himself away.

He separated himself from his feelings. Nothing good came of clouded judgment. She wouldn't risk running. There were too many families. Too many children. If Van started firing in this crowd, he'd kill someone for certain, though he'd never escape. Not through the congested parking lot. Corbin forced a calm he didn't feel. He'd have to bide his time for a better opportunity.

When the two were forced to stop for a clanging, steam-blowing train full of waving kids, he risked moving closer.

"Where's your boyfriend?" Van demanded.

The man turned, and Corbin easily sidestepped behind a lanky teen.

"He's, um, gone," Beth said.

"Gone where?"

Van pulled her near the cheerful red barn of a petting zoo and retrieved his phone.

The teenagers kept walking. Corbin quickly ducked behind the barn door. A goat butted against his pant leg, and he absently scratched the animal behind the ears. He angled his head, and the slots in the door provided a narrow view of the two.

Van typed something on his phone. Alerting his partner, most likely.

"After the train station," Beth said, "my boyfriend got nervous. We had a fight. He took off."

Clever ploy. They'd be less alert if they thought she was alone.

"How'd you find me?" she asked.

"Got lucky," Van replied. "Had to ditch the car, though. Someone called in an APB on the plates."

They knew they'd been made. They were definitely paying off someone low level in law enforcement. But they were still attempting to finish the job. Corbin stored that nugget of information for future reference.

"What's your angle, lady?" Van demanded, his gaze focused on the glowing screen in his palm. "I thought you were going to the Feds until I realized you checked into the hotel under an assumed name. What are you after? Blackmail?"

"I don't know what you're talking about."

"Don't make this hard on yourself. I need to know who you talked to. Who else did you share the information with? Did you tell your boyfriend about us after the train station?"

"I didn't tell him anything," she replied, a heart-wrenching tremor of fear in her voice.

The goat nibbled on the hem of his coat. Corbin glared, but the animal only bleated in return. He resumed petting, and the bleating stopped.

"Blackmailer," he muttered.

Van stowed his phone in his pocket and urged her back into the crowd. With no rowdy teenagers readily apparent, Corbin made do with a pack of family members laughing and pulling toddler-filled red wagons in a chaotic line.

Keeping pace proved easy. Van was in no hurry to exit the festival. Which was good since the family providing Corbin his cover was progressing with all the direction and purpose of a herd of cats. He bided his time, following within a safe distance. Van seemed to have taken Beth at her word. He wasn't keeping a very sharp vigil. Corbin wasn't exactly making himself invisible.

One of the toddlers in the group ahead of him dropped a stuffed bunny. Corbin ducked and retrieved the toy, then jogged to catch up. The toddler grinned and snatched the battered bunny with one chubby fist, stuffing the other in his mouth. The mother thanked Corbin before tugging her child in the opposite direction. As they passed several attractions, the crowds started to thin. Corbin hung farther back. The spots for cover were growing scarce. All Van had to do was turn around, and he'd easily spot someone tailing him.

Corbin was going to have to make his move soon.

The reason for the smaller crowds soon became apparent. A large sign reading Maze Closed Due to Weather blocked their path. A tower of hay bales marked the entrance, and Van dragged Beth behind the display.

Corbin glanced around. This was his last chance. He wasn't risking gunfire, though. Not unless it was absolutely necessary.

Van didn't know that. Corbin yanked his weapon from the holster. He edged around the stack of hay bales. Voices sounded.

He couldn't wait. The second man would arrive any minute, and a second man lowered his odds of success.

Taking a deep breath, he considered his options. He'd have to launch himself and hope that if Van fired, the shot would go wide. In the unfortunate circumstances he was hit, at least the bullet wouldn't take him down immediately. All he had to do was stay on his feet long enough to reach Van. Long enough to get off his own shot, if necessary.

He whipped around the corner. Beth caught sight of him first and jerked away.

Van swung around to confront Corbin, but it was already too late. Corbin was halfway to his goal.

Caught off balance, Van stumbled. His hand flailed, bringing the gun around. Too slow. Corbin's momentum carried him forward. The two struggled. He pulled away and cracked his pistol across the man's temple. Van crumpled, one hand clutching Beth's arm, dragging her down with him.

Then there was silence. Absolute. Deafening silence. His breath caught in his throat, and he patted his chest. Van hadn't had time to pull the trigger. Corbin went down on one knee. He kicked away the gun and reached for Beth.

She clutched his arm, her face turned away. The fragile defenses he'd erected collapsed. He wanted to take her somewhere he knew she would be safe. Anywhere but here. He wanted to hold her so close that nothing could ever harm her. He wanted to protect, shield her, keep her by his side.

He realized his hands were shaking with the force of emotion pouring through him.

All the barriers he'd put in place between his

feelings and his actions crumbled. There was nothing left. Nothing holding back the tide of longing. He'd been denying himself for so long, the emotions were overpowering.

He loosened his hold and set her away from him, tightening his hands into fists. Focus. He needed to focus. They were still vulnerable. Beth was still at risk. This place was crawling with families and children.

Worry clouded her face. "Are you all right?" she asked.

Great. Now she was asking him if *he* was all right. He had some serious soul-searching to do after this was all over.

He schooled his expression. "Fine. You?"

"I think so." She glanced around. "We have to get out of here. The other one is coming. Van texted him. He's meeting him here."

Corbin searched for a viable exit. They needed cover. They needed to circle back to the car. The most obvious exit provided neither. He wasn't risking any bystanders.

Van groaned and stirred. They were running out of time.

"My kingdom for a pair of handcuffs," Corbin muttered.

There was no way to disable the man.

Beth focused on something in the distance and

paled. "I think I see the other one. He's coming right toward us."

"C'mon. We'll take the maze."

"The maze?"

"It's good cover. And it's closed. No civilians."

"Fine. But you should know I have a terrible sense of direction. I once got lost in a shopping mall."

Her nervous chatter was almost comforting, and he fell back on his training. Anticipate the enemies' movements, evaluate a counterattack.

"Stay close," he ordered gently.

Together they skirted around the barrier. The stalks were tall, towering at least two feet over them, and the color of burlap. The leaves were dense, providing good cover, though the ground was slick from the recent frost.

Corbin dodged around a corner and ducked left, Beth close on his heels. They came to a dead end and halted.

Someone was crashing through the stalks near them. Corbin gripped her hand and they plunged through the tall stalks in the opposite direction. The crisp, dry leaves sounded like cannon fire, signaling their location. The maze was too overgrown. The paths hadn't been cleared well.

Beth turned one way, and he tugged on her hand. "No. We can't go toward the festival grounds. We have to lead them away in case they start shooting."

"I told you I had a bad sense of direction."

"Let's go," he said.

They ran down an aisle and someone burst on to the trail before them. Raynor. Corbin's heart jerked in his chest. Raynor aimed his gun at them, and Corbin dove to the side, shielding Beth with his body.

The bullet tore through the leaves above him, raining bits of burlap-colored leaves over their heads. He forced air into his lungs and assumed a calm he didn't feel. Shooting at a moving target was harder than it looked in the movies. They had the advantage.

Together they raced down the path and wove their way deeper into the maze. After a few minutes, they emerged into a large, open area with a two-story tower in the center that overlooked the maze.

"I'm going to see if I can spot him," he said. "I should be able to search the whole maze from that tower."

"Then I'm coming with you."

"Fine. But stay low."

The slats were close together on the railing in deference to small children, providing them with good cover. They maneuvered up the stairs and crouched. Acres of corn slashed with zigzagging paths stretched out before them to dizzying lengths. The maze was enormous. The sign had advertised ten acres. Corbin scanned the rows, searching for any sign of movement.

"There." Beth pointed. "I see him."

"Got it."

Raynor was a distance away, the rustle of leaves marking the man's position.

"He's lost track of us," Corbin said.

His heart hammered against his ribs. The first thing that had gone right today. He scanned the area. They'd have to regroup. Raynor couldn't leave Van sprawled in the open for long. He wouldn't want security barreling down on them. He'd know by now it was nearly impossible to find them in the maze.

Beth shivered beside him. "What next?"

Corbin scooted to the opposite edge of the platform and studied their options. The maze was bracketed by the interstate in the distance, green space and the fairgrounds. All exits forced them into the open.

He caught sight of the Moaning River to the north. "C'mon. I have an idea."

"Is it a good idea?"

"How well can you swim?"

She cast him a withering glare. "Sounds like a bad idea to me."

"The worst."

Her half grin was resigned. She trusted him, and this time he wasn't going to let her down.

* * *

The minute they entered the maze once more, Beth immediately became turned around. The realization left her dizzy and disoriented. She had no idea which direction they were running, whether they were going away from or toward the festival grounds. Thankfully, Corbin didn't appear to have the same problem. He navigated the twists and turns as though he was following a set path.

He paused once, his brow furrowed, then set off again with confident steps. The maze was eerily quiet beyond the soft thumps of their shoes hitting the hard earth path, and the rustle of the leaves catching their clothing.

After several minutes of running, a stitch formed in her side and she slowed.

Corbin turned, his expression concerned. "Are you all right?"

Pressing her fingers into the pain, she straightened. "Fine."

"Hang in there."

"Don't worry about me."

She sucked in a lungful of cold air and shook out her hands. She hadn't been monitoring her breathing. A rookie mistake.

Corbin reversed direction, shoving Beth gently ahead of him. They went back the direction they came. Stalks blocked their path, and she batted them aside. Her breath sounded harsh in her ears, and she had trouble keeping traction on the path.

They turned left and startled a flock of birds. Wings flapped, and she covered her face with her hands.

"This way," Corbin urged.

"Do you know where you're going?"

"Sort of. I think."

At least now she sympathized with all those victims in horror movies. She expected one of the goons to leap out at any moment. She couldn't tell if they were running from the danger or toward it. They came to a dead end and stopped.

Corbin looked left and right.

"Which way."

He pointed straight ahead. "That way."

Corbin plunged through the wall of corn. Beth paused only a moment. Though she knew it was only corn, years of conditioning had her following the path. She dove through the tall stalks, emerging on the other side, then gazed in wonder. It was like entering another world. They stood on a narrow patch of land separating the corn maze from the tree-lined Moaning River. Or creek. It wasn't much of a river, despite the auspicious title.

Corbin shoved the dry leaves together, disguising their forced exit.

She glanced around. "What now?"

"We listen."

Together they crouched near the edge of the maze. Voices sounded. The men were crashing through the cornstalks, calling to each other.

Her ears buzzed. The maze was huge. Acres of paths. And yet they could hear the men. Which meant they must be close.

Corbin glanced behind them. "Let's make for the creek bed. It'll lead us back to the fairgrounds."

"All right."

He rubbed the pad of his thumb over her cheek. "You've got a scratch."

She touched the spot and glanced at the drop of blood on her fingertips. "Those leaves are sharp."

His gaze focused, and she immediately went quiet. The air around them was eerily still.

A gunshot whizzed over her head, cutting the leaves above her.

Beth stifled a shriek and threw her arms over her face.

Corbin crouched over her, covering her with his body. "They can't see us. They're shooting blind."

Another bullet whizzed to the right of them and struck a tree in the distance.

Keeping low, they frog-walked toward the creek bed. Corbin turned around, brushing over their footsteps in a hasty attempt to disguise their path. He slipped down the side of the embankment, then held out his hand for her to follow.

She grasped his fingers and trailed him down the muddy slope. The heavy rains had eroded the embankment, turning the ground concave above them. Her feet were freezing, but this wasn't the time to complain. Not with those two goons hot on their heels.

She started toward the water, and Corbin swung her around. He shook his head, pointing above them.

She stilled.

Voices sounded.

"Can you see them?" one man called.

"No. I can't see them. I can't see nothing," the second man replied.

Beth froze. Corbin yanked her beneath the concave overhang. The men must have emerged from the maze. She held her breath, willing them to move on, but their voices ebbed and flowed above her.

"Be quiet," one of the men called. "I think I hear something."

Footsteps sounded, and dirt showered over them. The loamy scent of earth tickled her nose. She pressed her face against Corbin's jacket. His hands tightened around her. Water washing over pebbles in the creek disguised the sounds of their breathing.

"They didn't make it as far as the creek," the

man above them called. "They must still be in the maze."

Moisture soaked through her shoes and sent her shivering. She offered a brief prayer that the men wouldn't investigate any further. Their hiding spot wasn't the best. Corbin chafed her arms, and she melted into his warmth. Right then she didn't care about his professional rules. She needed his comforting strength. She pressed her ear against his heart, reassured by the steady, beating rhythm.

After what seemed like an hour, but was more like fifteen minutes, Corbin leaned back. "I think we can risk moving now. I'll check to be sure."

"Be careful."

He scooted from his cover and made his way up the embankment. His shoes slipped, and he grasped a tree root. Beth cringed. No shot sounded. No voices called.

He turned, half walking, half sliding down the muddy embankment. "I didn't see anything. We should get going."

"Where?"

"Out through the festival. It's still the safest. More people are better. Plenty of cover. They won't try for both of us under those conditions."

She took a cautious step, and mud oozed over the edges of her brand-new sneakers. Right then, she didn't care where they went as long as no one was shooting at them, and she could dry her feet.

Her shoes were a lost cause. She'd have to pitch them after this little adventure.

The steep banks forced them to navigate the creek in spots. The water was icy, and she sank up to her ankles in several places. Mud coated her hands and darkened her sleeves when she grasped the embankment for balance. They walked single file, toward the voices of the fairground.

Noises from the petting zoo sounded over the rushing stream, and Corbin jerked his head. "C'mon. We're near enough to the crowds. We can leave that way."

"Anything that gets me out of this mud."

"You first."

She started up the embankment and immediately realized why he'd insisted she go first. He braced his hands against her back and propelled her up the hill. She staggered away from the creek and leaned against a tall poplar tree.

Corbin followed close behind.

Chattering families walked the path not ten feet from them, but most people kept their eyes forward, completely oblivious to the two disheveled people catching their breath on the banks of the Moaning River.

Corbin dusted his hands together and grimaced. "I think we're safe. We might as well make for the car."

Hand in hand, they stumbled through the crowds.

Her feet were so cold, they were numb. She was moving on instinct and muscle memory alone. She couldn't feel her legs below the knee.

Their awkward appearance incited plenty of curious stares. She held her head high. Any other time she'd have been mortified. Not today. Today she was alive. She'd survived her third attack. Today she didn't care what people thought.

Corbin remained alert, but there was no sign of the two men. If there was any justice, they were following the sailing tracker to someplace horrid. Maybe the creek passed near a waste dump or a feedlot. They were far enough outside the suburbs to make that possible.

As they passed through the exit, the security guard glared at them.

Corbin tipped his head. "Good day."

Beth stifled a giggle.

They reached the car without incident, and she poured herself on to the seat. She leaned against the headrest and tilted her face toward Corbin.

"Thank you," Beth said.

Corbin paused, his fingers on the key in the ignition. "For what?"

She blinked rapidly. "For saving my life. For protecting me even though I didn't give you much reason to trust me."

He rested his hand on her shoulder. "You're going to be all right. I promise."

"Next time, I'll trust you sooner."

She turned to stare out the window lest he see the emotion in her expression.

Tuesday was coming soon. Her throat tightened. There wasn't going to be a next time.

ELEVEN

The hotel clerk eyed the two of them with thinly veiled derision. "No vacancies."

Not that Corbin could blame the man. They were coated head to toe in partially dried mud. Though they'd thoroughly wiped their shoes on the mat outside the door, there was a halo of dirt surrounding their feet.

He peeled a hundred bill from the top of his stack. "How about now?"

"Might have something." The whip-thin man scratched his brittle, gray whiskers. "But I don't want no trouble. And I don't want my towels getting all messed up. You clean up after yourselves, and you leave the room clean."

"Rooms. Plural," Corbin corrected. "We'll take *two* adjoining rooms."

The man lifted a bushy gray eyebrow in question. "You're awful fancy for a couple of folks who look like they've been wallowing in a pig sty."

Corbin peeled off another hundred-dollar bill.

He was cold, wet, hungry, dirty and at the end of his patience with judgmental front desk clerks. This hotel room was costing a fortune considering the state of the premises, and he didn't care if he was ever reimbursed.

Right then, he'd pay a thousand dollars for a hot shower. "Two rooms. No questions. We'll leave your towels as pure as the driven snow."

The man unsnapped the breast pocket of his red-checked shirt and tucked the bills inside. "All righty, then." He retrieved two actual keys with plastic tabs from a Peg-Board behind the counter. "You're in rooms 222 and 224."

The hotel Corbin had chosen was just across the Wisconsin border. Though he'd called the police to update them on the two men, and despite the fact they'd ditched the tracker, he wanted some space between Beth and the most recent attack.

They were starting over. Setting everything to zero.

He palmed the two keys. Not exactly the most secure arrangement, but beggars couldn't be choosers, and they were looking like a couple of beggars right then.

Their feet dragging, their shoes dropping dirt clods, they made their way up the concrete stairs to their adjoining rooms. The motel had seen better days, though someone had taken the trouble to repaint the exterior a jolting shade of purple.

A police cruiser slowly drove past. Homeland Security had requested local assistance while they mustered a security team. Three attempts on her life in two days had finally gotten Beth government-sanctioned protection—even without proof of her evidence. Corbin grunted. Better late than never.

She leaned heavily against the wall. "I'm so tired, I think I'm going to die."

He knew the feeling. Reaching behind her, he keyed open the door, and she stepped inside. She staggered the distance and collapsed face-first on the nearest bed, her arms akimbo.

"Wake me when this is all over," she declared, her voice muffled.

He tossed her meager bag of belongings on to the mauve bedspread beside her. "Take a hot shower. Get some rest."

She flopped on to her back, splaying her hands. "You, too."

Corbin offered a wry smile "Will do. You hungry?"

"No. I don't want to think about anything but getting clean, and then sleeping for a week."

He knew the feeling. "I'll check back later."

He spent twenty minutes in the shower. When he emerged, the mirror was completely fogged over. He wiped a space and stared at himself. He'd looked worse. There were times in Afghanistan when he'd gone over a week without a shower. In the heat of summer. In weather that would scorch the bark off a tree.

He'd looked better, too. A lot better. He tore the tags off his new clothing and donned a pair of jeans and a zip-front athletic shirt. He yanked new socks over his feet and collapsed on the bed. He'd been tired before. But he couldn't remember being this tired.

He must have dozed, because when he jerked awake, the time on the clock was past dinner.

His stomach growled. Neither of them had eaten in hours. He dragged himself upright and ran his fingers through his hair. He flipped through the binder on the nightstand and discovered a nearby pizza joint. He ordered two different varieties and added a dessert for good measure. A chocolate brownie. Beth had a weakness for chocolate.

The pizza shop didn't offer delivery, but at least it was close by. With the patrol car still on duty, he drove the distance, then parked back at the hotel. The boxes balanced on his palm, he climbed the stairs two at a time. If he slowed down, the fatigue might return, but as long as he kept moving, he was fine.

He returned to his room and considered whether to disturb Beth and risk waking her. Thankfully, the walls were thin, and he heard the TV as well as footsteps. She was awake.

He knocked softly on the adjoining door and announced, "It's Corbin," then mentally slapped his forehead. Who else would it be?

The security chain scraped across metal, and he smiled. At least she'd had the presence of mind to set the extra security.

He extended a flat box. "Pizza. There's a shop close by. And just to show that I'm not a cheap date." He reached in his pocket and retrieved a can. "I got us each a soda out of the machine."

She offered a weary smile. "I'm starving. You're a dear."

"Pizza cures all ills."

"Do you ever skip meals?"

"Not if I can help it." He set the box on the small side table, flipped open the lid and retrieved a slice. "Low blood sugar means brain fog. I've got to stay sharp."

"Mmm." She took a slice. "Pepperoni. My favorite."

"Good. I figured pepperoni was safe enough. Let's see if we made the news."

Beth flipped on the TV. "Might as well see if I'm America's most wanted."

They watched the entire program, but there was nothing about a commotion at the Harvest Festival or a search for a missing accountant accused of embezzlement. Following the news, a movie featuring two strangers on a disastrous cross-country trip played.

Corbin hoisted an eyebrow. "Seems fitting."

"How far are we going to drive tomorrow?"

"Good news. No more driving. I've requested plane tickets back to Chicago as soon as we can get a flight out. Even without the evidence in hand, Homeland Security now considers you a high-value asset. They're willing to dispatch a unit rather than operating out of Virginia. They want to keep everything close to Quetech until this over. Third time's a charm in kidnapping."

Beth groaned and rubbed her face. "We're going back to Chicago? I can't believe I spent all that time and money getting out of Chicago for nothing."

"We've gone over this all before. You could have gone to the FBI first."

She flashed a grin. "Think of all the fun you'd have missed if I'd done the sensible thing."

"The past couple of days certainly haven't been boring." He glanced at her. Everything changed after today. He was no longer operating solo. She'd be part of the Homeland Security juggernaut once they landed in Chicago.

The phone rang, and Corbin checked the number before answering.

"Thank me," a familiar voice ordered.

"Thank you, Baker."

"You're welcome," Baker barked gruffly. "I got an emergency review. You're heading up the case. You and the accountant can hunker down in Chicago while we sort out the information from Quetech."

"Thank you."

"You owe me. I had to go out on a limb considering we got nothing in the way of proof from your accountant. You getting shot at really helped speed up the paperwork."

"Anytime."

"I've got a line on your two stalkers. We haven't caught up to them yet, but we will. The video footage was run through facial identification, and we got two solid hits on identification. The names are Van Gardiner and Doug Raynor. A couple of mercenaries left over from the war on terror. Those two guys are connected to some very bad stuff. But they're just the cleanup crew. They're for hire. They got nothing to do with the big picture."

"I kinda guessed that."

"Remember that bombing in Myanmar?"

Corbin glanced at Beth and nodded. "Yeah. Fifty-one dead. Another hundred or so wounded?"

"That's the one. Looks like they're trying to bring their terrorist cell stateside. Shock and awe. If we can get evidence on the money laundering, we can trace the source. Everyone gets a Christmas bonus, and no one dies. Simple. I like simple."

"What's next?"

"Once the evidence arrives, I'll get you back to headquarters in style. First class. Hot towels. The whole nine yards."

"I'll settle for something that doesn't smell like wet dog." The air freshener in the Honda wasn't holding up so well. "Where are we setting up in Chicago?"

"The accountant's apartment building."

"Is that wise?"

"There's a vacant apartment on her floor. If they come for her, we'll be waiting."

"No." Echoes of the FBI haunted Corbin. "Out of the question. I'm not using her as bait."

"I didn't say we were. I just said that if they come, we'll be waiting."

"Is there a difference?"

"As far as you know, yes, there's a difference." The line crackled. "Your accountant is a high-value asset. That means she's under our protection. With all the rights and privileges that status entitles."

As in, *hands off.* Corbin read the undercurrent. "Got it."

"You'll be out of Chicago by the end of the week. We'll have a team in place by the time you two get there."

"Good."

"Everything staying professional out there?"

The implication was clear. Beth was part of an investigation. Corbin had a responsibility to maintain a personal distance. "Yep."

"Keep it that way."

He hung up the phone and glanced at Beth. "We've got confirmation on the security detail. You're going home."

Her expression was tight. "What about you? What happens now?"

"I'm in charge until this is finished."

"Congratulations." The patina in her leaf-green eyes had lost some of its luster. "You'll be home before you know it."

His stomach dipped, and the past few years caught up to him in a flash. He didn't have a home. Not really. Neither of them did. They were nomads, though not by nature. They were both trying to outrun the loneliness. They were both trying to outrun grief. Near as he could tell, they were both failing miserably.

So much of his life had been a reflection of Evan. Keeping up with Evan. Trying to be like Evan. He'd defined himself by how he compared, and with nothing tying him to that standard, he'd gone adrift. He was like an actor in a stage play who was still saying his lines even though one of the characters was missing. He was hitting his marks and going through the motions, but he was alone. Emoting to an empty space.

Snippets of conversation fell into place like pieces in a puzzle. Beth had been close to her dad. She'd cared for him when he was sick. Corbin had no doubt she'd taken over the role of both parent and child in the relationship toward the end. That's often how lengthy illness worked. He'd seen as much when his grandparents were ill.

She was trying to outwit her grief by never staying in one place long enough for the feelings to manifest. They were both fighting the same battle, and there was nothing he could do to help her. He was bound by professional ethics and a code of conduct. The lines had blurred over the past few days, but that didn't change his responsibility.

No matter what his feelings, Elizabeth Greenwood was off-limits.

Corbin couldn't quite meet the sadness in her eyes. "Don't worry, you'll be back to your old life in no time."

She glanced away. "You'll forget all about me."

"Never," he replied, his voice husky.

A heavy weight settled on his chest. He'd found the key to his future, but it belonged to the one doorway he was forbidden to enter.

By Tuesday morning, Beth's Chicago apartment seemed a lot smaller with the swarming government agents. Her heel tapping lightly against the floor, she followed the steady tick, tick, tick of the second hand on the clock. Almost time. She was a few seconds away from vindication.

She glanced at Corbin, his feet propped on the ottoman, his face highlighted by the glow of the computer screen. Something had changed between them. Somewhere between Minneapolis and Chicago, he'd become little more than a stranger.

One of the milling agents poured himself a cup of coffee from the carafe on the counter. From the moment Corbin had hung up the phone following the attack in the corn maze, a sense of urgency had prevailed. The information Homeland Security had received on Van Gardiner and Doug Raynor had set in motion a chain of events that had them barreling toward a conclusion.

The additional agents were treating her with cautious courtesy. Polite. Professional. Reserved. She hadn't officially been moved from the "suspect" column to the "cooperating" column just yet. Everything hinged on that email.

She might have attributed Corbin's change of attitude to the presence of the other agents, but the shift had started well before their arrival. The shift had happened after the phone call.

She rubbed her eyes and stifled a yawn. This was better. His detachment was a good thing. They both traveled extensively for their jobs. They were both dedicated to their work. There was no middle ground between them. She'd always take second place to his job, and she deserved more. She deserved to be first in his life. She wasn't settling.

One good thing had come of her time with Quetech. She'd discovered new wells of courage within herself, and she was done playing it safe all the time. Things were going to be different from now on. She'd been adrift for too long. She loved her work, but she was unsatisfied.

When this was all over, she was going to do some serious soul-searching about the direction of her life. It was time to reconnect with friends. It was time to reconnect with the things that brought her joy. It was time to find out what exactly brought her joy. She was going to volunteer more at church. She was going to become a part of the community once more rather than a vagabond drifting through for Sunday services.

Corbin caught her gaze. "How are you holding up?"

"Good."

Terrible, actually. She was on pins and needles. The buzzing of Corbin's phone startled them both. He set his computer aside, rose from the couch and took the call on the balcony. The sliding doors closed. He paced. His free hand gestured. His expression grew intense.

She glanced at the clock, and her stomach

pitched. The email should have arrived by now. The conversation continued. She'd even made allowances for the shift in time zones. Something didn't feel right.

Twenty minutes later, Corbin returned inside.

"What's wrong?" she demanded. "What happened?"

"That was Agent Keel," he said, his voice grim. "From the FBI. Your email didn't arrive."

"But—" she checked the clock again "—it's time."

"Maybe you got the time wrong."

"No. I didn't. I didn't get the time wrong." She clutched her head and paced the room. "I set the date…"

Her hands dropped to her sides. She'd been keying in the numbers when she heard something. Her mouse had shot off the desk. She'd clicked quickly through the screens.

"Wait. I need to check something." She flipped open the lid to her laptop and keyed in her password. The spinning circle rotated. "C'mon. Hurry up and load, you stupid thing."

The coffee-drinking agent leaned his hip against the counter. She couldn't remember his name. She couldn't tell any of them apart. They all wore the same dark suits and had the same crisp haircut.

"Here we go." She clicked through the screens

and opened her email, then clicked on the confirmation from No Going Back. Her heart plummeted. "I don't understand."

"What?" Corbin leaned over her shoulder. "What's wrong?"

"Everything is correct." She pushed up the cuffs of her sleeves and typed through more screens. "I don't understand why the email wasn't delivered."

Nausea churned in her stomach, and the room seemed to blur and fade. This was bad. This was very bad. Everything hinged on that email. Her whole future. Corbin's reputation. He'd stuck out his neck for her. She was telling the truth, but who'd believe her? She doubted she'd believe herself in the same situation.

"All right," Corbin said, his voice measured. "Let's think this through. Let's work the problem."

The coffee-drinking agent exchanged a glance with his partner. Her cheeks burned. She was firmly entrenched in the "suspect" column.

Corbin's phone buzzed again. He glanced at the number and stepped onto the balcony once more. Her limbs felt as though they were weighted.

What had gone wrong? She had to think. She had to retrace her steps. Quetech was paranoid. Every electronic message passed through their computer servers. Every. Single. One. She recalled hearing about someone in the company who'd sent salary information to his personal account from a Quetech email. A filter had caught the infraction, and he'd been fired. Had her email gotten caught in one of those filters? Perhaps something in the text—a word or a file number—had triggered a response.

She paced, a hand pressed over her stomach. This couldn't be happening. Of all the stupid, idiotic mistakes. Why hadn't she simply dropped a flash drive in an actual mailbox? Somehow sending an email had seemed less larcenous. Less invasive.

She'd planned everything. *Think about your disappearance at least as much as you thought about what put you on the run in the first place.* She'd done her homework. She'd considered all the angles. Despite her careful planning, thus far, not one thing had gone as planned. She'd nearly gotten kidnapped on her way out of the building, Corbin had followed her on the train, and the email had never arrived.

There had to be another way to retrieve the information. She sat down at the computer and pulled up No Going Back once more. She keyed through all the screens, and even wrote a frantic message to the help desk. According to their records, the email had been triggered.

Where was it then? Why wasn't Agent Keel opening the attachment?

She glanced at the balcony. Was this some sort

of test? Probably not. There was too much whispering. Too many hooded glances from the other agents. They were looking at Corbin and back at her. Her stomach churned.

They must assume that she'd conned him.

Corbin appeared once more, his face grim. "We're dead in the water."

"What do you mean?" she asked, sensing a shift.

"We don't have enough evidence for a warrant on Quetech."

"But, but... I don't understand. What happens now?"

He pinched the bridge of his nose. "It's not your fault, Beth. Near as I can figure, they had a filter—what we call a sniffer—on one of the computer servers, and something in your email triggered the net. The sniffer is constantly searching out specific words and characters. The email was most likely quarantined and flagged for review, which alerted someone at Quetech that you were on to them. That means we have to go about this the old-fashioned way. We find a judge and make our case."

"Then...nothing?"

"They've outmaneuvered us, and they know it. By the time we get a warrant, everything will be scrapped." He whipped off his glasses and absently polished the lenses. "Maybe they'll get careless. We'll keep monitoring Cayman Holdings. Look for another chance."

There wasn't going to be another chance, and they both knew it. If Quetech had intercepted her email, then they knew by now that someone had discovered the money laundering. They'd be destroying the evidence and covering their tracks.

She sprang to her feet. "Why were they still coming after me? They obviously knew about the email."

"To clean up the loose ends. To ensure you didn't have a copy." For the first time since arriving in Chicago, he met her gaze, his expression unguarded. "Don't worry. You'll still have protection from the marshals. Just until we know for certain you're safe."

"I don't care about the protection." She'd agreed to witness protection until the case went to trial. "There has to be another way."

"You tried, Beth." Corbin placed a hand on her shoulder. "No one blames you."

The coffee-drinking agent reached for a donut from the box on the counter. "That's it, then? We packing up here?"

"No." Beth frantically shook her head. "I'll go back. I'll copy the information to an external drive. This isn't over."

Corbin held up his hands. "I can't ask you to

do that. Too dangerous. Someone on the inside of Quetech knows about you. They tracked you."

"They don't suspect you." She snapped her fingers. "I can tell you what to do."

"I can't. Not without the proper authority. Employees, like you, are protected by the Whistleblower Act. I'd need a warrant. I'd need to move through regular channels."

"This isn't over." As the plan formulated in her mind, her resolve firmed. "I'll go in early. I'll be in and out before anyone suspects."

"There are too many variables," came Corbin's immediate, uncompromising response. "And not enough time to account for them all. I'd need days, not hours, to put something this complex together."

"We can't wait that long. Once the bank opens, they'll start deleting records." She frantically considered the timeline. "Think about it. Quetech is the last place they'll be looking for me. I don't need much time. Twenty minutes. A half hour at most. By the time they figure out I'm there, I'll be gone."

Corbin flattened his hand against the back of his head. "They'll have changed your password by now."

"I don't think so. Everyone left early on Friday, remember? Ted from IT was leaving for the weekend. There wasn't anyone there who knows how to change a password."

"You might be right. You didn't send the email until after three."

Hope flared in her chest. She felt his resistance faltering. He was softening to the idea. "No one pays attention to temporary employees."

The coffee-drinking agent raised his hand to get their attention. "Can't we just send her in now? While the place is empty?"

"No," Corbin muttered darkly. "The company is paranoid. No employees in or out unless security is on site. Miss Greenwood won't be able to enter the building outside of regular working hours."

Her throat tightened. *Miss Greenwood.* Her status change was permanent. He wasn't even using her first name anymore.

He'd trusted her. He'd kept her safe. She wasn't letting him down.

"See?" she said. "My idea is perfect."

"Nope. Too dangerous. We still haven't gotten a warrant for the security footage inside the building. We don't know who planted the tracking device on you."

Beth slammed shut the lid on her laptop. "According to Human Resources, you still work there, too, Agent Ross." His expression flickered at her use of his title, and she experienced an entirely selfish twinge of victory. Two could play at that game. "You said it yourself—they're not looking for you. You can be my protection."

"That hasn't worked out too well so far."

The bitterness in his voice cut her to the quick. He thought he'd failed her, but she'd failed him. All he'd done was believe in her when no one else did.

"We're here, aren't we? It's worked out well enough." She rose and approached him, standing toe to toe, willing him to understand. "I need to do this. I have to do this."

For him. For herself. For Timothy. For her dad. She wasn't backing down. Not when they were this close to tracing the source. He wouldn't regret trusting her. Not if she could help it.

Corbin flipped back his jacket and planted his hands on his hips. "Can I speak with you outside, Miss Greenwood?"

She gave a silent prizefighter cheer with her clenched hands. She had him. He was softening. He was going to agree.

The two agents exchanged a glance.

"Sure," Beth said, dropping her hands.

Best not to be too obvious.

Corbin led her into the corridor and raked his hands through his hair again. "How much time do you need?"

"Not much. Like I said. Twenty minutes. I know what I'm looking for this time."

Crossing his arms, he paced the narrow space. "I can't give you much protection. Legally, my hands are tied. As an undercover operative, I'm walking a very narrow line. Anything I do in the retrieval of the information risks blowing the case in court."

A steady calm took hold of her. "I know. But you said it yourself, I'm not bound by those rules. I'm the whistle-blower, remember?"

Corbin gently grasped her face in his hands, his thumb brushing gently along her temple. "The decisions I made in this case have put you in danger. I can't risk doing that again."

Beth blinked rapidly. He was still trying to protect her. She was falling in love with him, but she'd sort her feelings out later. She feared she'd moved past the tipping point. Even if she opened herself up to dating again, she'd never find anyone who measured up to him, and she wasn't prepared to settle.

For now, she had to prove to him that his trust was not misplaced.

He made a sound of frustration. "Look, I'm sorry about how I behaved these past few days. I let things get out of hand. I, uh, have a professional responsibility."

"We have feelings for each other." Swallowing around the lump in her throat, she gathered her courage. "There's nothing wrong with that."

"I can't—"

"We don't have to act on those feelings." Her voice was strong. Confident. She was getting better at this all the time. "We're both adults. Neither of us is going to change, and that's all right."

"I'm in charge of this case. You're off-limits. There can't be anything between us. I'm sorry."

She hadn't thought he could wrench any more pain from her heart, but his words cut her to the core. He had choices. They both did. He was intentionally barring himself from her. He was intentionally barring his heart from her.

She sucked in a breath. "You have nothing to be sorry about. This was never going to work, and that's all right. Some things don't. That's life."

There was a part of her that hoped he'd say they could get together when this was all over. A naive, romantic part of her. But that was a foolish thought. Deep in her heart, she'd known that all along. He wouldn't wait for her because time wasn't the problem.

He heaved a breath. "You don't have to do this. We'll find another way."

They'd both see this through, no matter the personal cost.

"I have to do this," she said. "For Timothy. For Sam."

Corbin's jaw worked. He dropped his hands to his sides and backed away. "All right. We go to work as usual. Both of us. But it's my call. At the first sign of trouble, it's over. No arguments. Understood?"

She could love this man.

The pain nearly took her breath away. She bit down hard to keep her chin from quivering. She could easily see them spending the rest of their lives together. He was not indifferent to her. Even as he tried to distance himself, his actions showed another side of him. He cared more than he was willing to admit, but he'd always be holding a part of himself back.

She rose on her tiptoes and pressed a soft kiss against the rough stubble of his cheek. "Understood."

His arms tightened around her shoulders before dropping away. They'd officially said their goodbyes. Though the truth pained her, she was entitled to a man who had a heart and soul to commit to her.

She deserved more. She deserved his whole heart.

TWELVE

Corbin pulled onto a side street near Quetech and put the car in gear. He smoothed his tie and glanced at Beth. "I'll drop you off here. If we arrive together, we risk further speculation."

Everything he admired about her was on full display this morning. She was calm. She was composed. She was beautiful. She'd neatly alleviated him of all responsibility for anything that might have happened between them.

She'd spared him an awkward conversation and put their relationship back on solid footing. He should have been relieved.

She met his steady gaze without flinching. "All right."

Her eyes haunted him. She'd given him a chance at a future together.

She'd given him the opportunity to tell her that he'd wait for her. That they could be together when the case was finished and he was no longer bound by professional ethics.

In that instant she'd shattered all the notions he'd had of himself. She'd ripped apart all the plans he'd set in place for his future. But he couldn't change. He couldn't be the man she wanted. The man she needed. Though he'd nearly been undone by her touch, he'd rejected her offer.

Because in that moment he'd felt the consequences of his actions. Knowing someone close to him was in danger had filled him with a terrible emptiness. He'd known then there was no future between them.

Despite everything he knew in his heart, he wanted nothing more than to put the car in gear and drive until the past was nothing more than a distant memory.

Instead, he drummed his fingers on the steering wheel. "You know what happens after today, right?"

"Witness protection."

"Temporarily." They'd pushed everything into high gear. Calls had been made, and the marshals had agreed to the speedy timetable. She'd be under their protection from the moment she exited the building. "Just until we know it's safe. Might be a few weeks. Might be a few months. I can't make any guarantees."

She'd be safe. Everything else he left unsaid. He didn't tell her that he was falling in love with her. He didn't tell her that he wanted to be near her, every minute of every day. He didn't tell her that she'd left an indelible impression on his heart.

This way was better. Better to lose her now than risk losing his heart and soul to grief later.

"Don't worry," she said. "I knew what I was signing up for."

Now was the time for action. They'd said everything they needed to say.

He'd take a full breath when this was all over, and he knew she was safe in the hands of the marshals. "Get in and out of the building as quickly as possible. Speak with as few people as possible. You don't need to be rude, you're busy. Behind schedule. Holiday weekend put you behind."

"Got it."

"I'll run interference."

"I know you will."

Despite agreeing to everything, they remained in the car. Silent. Staring at the dashboard. Throughout the endless night, he'd come to a few troubling conclusions in the early hours of the morning. He wasn't protecting his parents from his job, he was protecting himself. He'd used the job as an excuse, but he was drifting apart from his family because he didn't know where he fit anymore.

Being together only reminded everyone that someone was missing. He'd chosen to abandon them instead. But what purpose did that serve?

Was he doing Evan's memory justice by destroying what was left of his family?

Instead of being there while they were grieving, he'd chosen the selfish path. He'd chosen to manage his pain privately.

The job was just an excuse. He was going to make some changes. He was going to be honest. Evan's death had changed them all. Their relationship was different. And that was okay. Different was neither better nor worse. Different was just, well, different.

Beth's smile was sad. "You're a good man, Corbin Ross."

He knew it then. This was goodbye. What he knew was right for both of them. Yet he felt as though he'd stepped off a cliff and was tumbling into an abyss. They'd see each other again, they'd have to. The case. But their relationship would be professional. Superficial.

Corbin swiveled in his seat. "There's something I want to do."

He'd faced armed men with less trepidation. He wouldn't burden her with his feelings, but he wanted her to know that she'd meant something to him. Something precious and important.

"What's that?" she asked.

"Can I kiss you?"

Her expression softened. "Always."

His heart constricted painfully in his chest. Her

mouth was so close, and when she shut her eyes and leaned toward him, he surrendered to a need that was more powerful than his good sense. Their lips met, and an unbearable yearning tightened in his chest. Her hands tangled in his hair, and his fingers caught on the silk of her blouse. The embrace was fierce and over too soon.

She pulled back and studied him, her gaze intense, as though memorizing his features. "Thank you. For everything." She tweaked his glasses. "You'll always be my superhero."

She was out of the car before he could speak.

His throat closed, and he fought back a wave of longing. He knew then that she was embedded in his heart and soul more deeply than he'd ever thought possible.

Beth frantically pulled up the files and attached them to the digital folder. She cast a surreptitious glance behind her, searching for Corbin, then faced forward.

Karli had cornered him with the news of Sam's death the moment he'd walked into the building. He'd been attempting to extract himself for the past fifteen minutes. Though Beth sensed his frustration, the encounter was actually proving useful, giving her time to accomplish her task.

As she hit the final key, a shadow appeared behind her.

Janice hovered in the doorway of the cubicle, her eyes red-rimmed, and her face pale. "Matt wants to see you."

Beth clicked a few keys. "I'm just finishing up here."

"He says now." Janice sniffled. "He says it's urgent."

Unease skittered along Beth's nerve endings. Matt had hired her. He must have suspected something. Sam's death probably had him frightened, but she wasn't allowed to tell him the FBI was involved until the information was safely out of the building. Which meant she had no words of reassurance for him. She was just a friendly neighborhood whistle-blower going about her business.

She yanked the flash drive from the USB port and tucked her key ring into her pocket. "I was sorry to hear about Sam."

"Me, too." Janice sniffled loudly. "I just can't believe it."

"Maybe you should go home."

"I might. I thought I'd feel better if I was here. But I don't."

Beth watched the devastated woman retreat down the corridor, her heart heavy. Such a waste. And for what? Greed. Plain and simple. No one at Quetech was fighting an ideological war. Someone had gotten greedy, and lives had been shattered.

She searched the empty corridor and bit back

her frustration. There was no sign of Corbin. She'd promised she wouldn't stray from her cubicle without telling him. He was paranoid enough without her disappearing.

Janice paused at the end of the corridor. "You better hurry," she said. "Matt doesn't like to be kept waiting."

Beth tugged her lower lip between her teeth. She'd make some excuse to Matt and leave immediately. Resisting Janice's order was bound to cause even more suspicion. The office was quiet, voices hushed. Everyone was on edge.

She followed Janice a few feet, then turned. "I forgot something. I'll be right back."

Once in her cubicle, she hastily scrawled two words: "Matt's office." Janice was sniffling her way back to her desk when Beth emerged once more. She tweaked her collar and strode down the corridor.

Matt's door was propped open, and he gestured her inside. "Can you close that?"

"Sure." She jerked her thumb toward the corridor. "I have a meeting in five."

The chief executive officer was handsome in a slick, frat boy kind of way, though she avoided him whenever possible. He had an aggressive sort of charm she attributed to his shorter-than-average stature. He was obsessed with working out and filled the breakroom refrigerator with food for his paleo diet. When he wasn't talking about his cardio routine, he was bragging about how much weight he could bench.

"Don't worry," he said. "This shouldn't take long."

She took the seat before his desk. He stood and circled toward her, then perched on the edge, his knees inches from hers. A twinge of anxiety settled in the pit of her stomach.

She plastered a grin on her face. "How can I help you, Matt?"

"Did you know that every email you send from this company goes through our computer servers? We flag certain information. Sensitive information."

He knew.

Her nerve endings buzzed, and her heel tapped against the floor. "Why did you ask me to audit the accounts if you knew what I'd find?"

His chuckle was hollow and grating. "I didn't hire you. Sam did."

The pieces fell together, and nausea rose in throat. "You lied to Janice, and Janice lied to me."

She'd never even questioned the information.

"Yep." He leaned over her, but she refused to cower from him. "You attempted to steal information from this company."

There was no use denying the truth. She smoothed

her quaking hands over her skirt. "I'm protected by the Whistle-blower Act."

He braced his hands on the desk, leaning back, and for the first time, she noticed he was sweating. "Pretty gutsy, coming back here to try again. But you have to understand, I can't let that happen."

"You can't touch me, Matt." She fisted her hand over her mouth and cleared her throat. "The FBI knows I'm here. If anything happens to me, you'll be implicated."

A bead of sweat dripped down the side of his face. "You're bluffing. If you'd been to the FBI, where are they? Security has orders to alert me of any visitors. We just have regular staff today. You're on your own. Are you wired?"

"N-no."

He tilted his head. "Strangely enough, I believe you."

His braced arms quaked. He wasn't nearly as confident as he was trying to let on. He wasn't a killer. He was middle management caught up in something over his head.

The sooner she left, the better.

"If that's all—" she stood "—I'll be going."

"No." He flipped open a box on his desk and brandished a pistol. "I'm sorry, Ms. Greenwood. I can't let you."

Her knees weakened, and she flashed her palms. "Don't do this, Matt."

"You don't understand." His voice cracked, and the gun wavered dangerously. He swiped at his forehead again. "I don't have a choice."

He wasn't a killer by nature, but he was desperate. Frightened. A volatile combination.

"How did this happen?" She sneaked a glance over her shoulder. The frosted windows prevented anyone from seeing anything but hazy shapes inside the closed office. "You can still get out. You're a good man. A kind man. There's nothing that can't be fixed. Think of your family."

"I didn't mean for any of this to happen." He gave an agitated shake of his head, revealing his thinning hairline. "It started small. I just needed some time to cover a bad investment. A bridge. But that's not how these things, work, is it? I was vulnerable when they approached. The guy didn't seem like a terrorist. I thought he was a low-level player looking to launder some drug money. No real harm in that, right? After one transaction, I was compromised. They had me on tape. They had a paper trail. They blackmailed me, I swear."

Her instincts were correct. He didn't want to do this, but he felt trapped. He wanted an escape. She had to find a way to give him one.

"Then go to the FBI." She took a cautious step back. "Tell them what you know. Make a deal."

"I can't." He swiped the back of his hand across the sweat beading his forehead. "I told them Sam was suspicious about what they were doing. They killed him. I've laundered money for terrorists. My reputation is shot. They'll lock me up and throw away the key. Or I'll be dead. I got no good choices. You gotta understand, Beth. I didn't have a choice. It's you or me. I've called in a couple of guys. They're coming for you."

Her breath caught. "Yeah. I've met them. You helped them plant the tracker on me, didn't you?"

"I just thought they were going to talk some sense into you. Maybe bribe you."

"You knew exactly what they were going to do."

Any sympathy for him died. He was saving himself. At any cost.

Matt was nervous. He was trying to build up the courage to commit murder. He couldn't shoot her. Not here. But she feared if she made any sudden moves, he'd act impulsively. He was clearly a desperate man at the end of his rope.

The fire alarm blared. Matt jumped, and nearly dropped the gun. She cringed, expecting him to accidentally pull the trigger.

"What's going on?" he demanded.

Corbin. Corbin had pulled the fire alarm.

"There must be a fire," she spoke calmly. "We need to exit the building."

"No. No. It has to be a drill." The gun dipped. "This is good. The building will empty. Fewer people, fewer witnesses. This is good."

Her heart thudded against her ribs. Her dad always said there was nothing more dangerous than a terrified man with a gun. Perspiration darkened the collar of his shirt. Matt Shazier had just turned into a very, very dangerous man.

The alarm blared, and her head throbbed. Panic threatened to overwhelm her, and she clenched her hands. No. She had to work the problem. She had to think. An unnatural calm came over her. The decisions she made during the next few minutes were going to be the difference between life and death.

She inhaled through her nose and exhaled through her mouth. "What are you going to do, Matt? What's your plan?"

He awkwardly shrugged out of his coat, switching the gun from hand to hand, then yanked on his tie. His desperation was palpable, raising the temperature of the room.

He glanced at the flashing red light on the ceiling. "Why don't they turn off that stupid alarm?"

An acrid scent teased her nostrils. "Do you smell that smoke? There's a real fire. We should go."

"But they're not here yet. I'm just supposed to hold you until they get here." Confusion and horror flitted across his features. "All right." Matt waved his gun. "Go. Open the door. Let's go. We'll take the stairs."

The alarm blared even louder outside his office, though the corridor was eerily empty.

A flash of movement near the stairwell caught her attention. Maybe Corbin. Maybe not. There was no way for him to signal her without alerting Matt.

They passed the coffee nook, and she quickly calculated her odds. She was alone. Matt had a gun. He was desperate.

Without giving herself time to think, she snatched a coffeepot from the warmer and swung wildly. The blow caught Matt on the temple. He shrieked. Glass shattered, and scalding liquid spilled over his hand. She released the handle and dove away.

Keeping low, she wove her way through the cubicles. As she passed an open space, a hand clamped over her mouth. She jerked around. Her heart leaped into her throat.

Tweedledumber.

He yanked her upright, the gun pressed against her temple. "Come out, come out wherever you are. I've got your girlfriend."

A familiar silhouette appeared from behind a partition wall. Corbin held his hands in the air. His gun dangled from his outstretched hand.

The man holding her yanked her back. "Set down the gun. Real easy."

"Let her go," Corbin said, his voice deadly calm. "This building is crawling with FBI. They're closing in on you."

"Then where are they?"

The warm breath panting against her ear made her shudder with revulsion.

"Where's your friend?" Corbin called.

"Out of commission, thanks to you." The man squeezed her painfully. "That's why this one is personal. I'm going to dump her into the river. I'm gonna make her suffer first."

Muffled thumps sounded from near the coffee nook. "Matt has a—"

Van cuffed her with the back of his hand, cutting off her warning.

"You'll never get out of the building, Van." Corbin rested his gun on the floor and straightened. "It's over."

"Like I said, this is personal."

"No!" Matt staggered into the space between them, his hand pressed to his forehead, blood streaming through his fingers. "No more. No more killing."

"Stay out of this, Shazier." Corbin motioned toward the injured man. "Get down."

Van leveled his gun. "You're the last loose end, Shazier. I have a message from the boss. Your services are no longer necessary."

Matt dove forward.

Beth clamped her hand around Van's arm, and he knocked her once more with his free hand. She staggered, the metallic taste of blood on her tongue, her lip throbbing.

A shot sounded, and Matt jerked. Beth dove away. The distraction gave Corbin the opening he needed. As though watching from a distance, she noted the moment he turned. His hand out-stretched. The flare from the barrel of the gun.

Another shot sounded, and Van collapsed.

Her knees gave out, and she dropped to the floor. Time seemed to decelerate, and she felt as though she was moving in slow motion. She noted the color of every thread in the carpet, the way the rough material felt against her palms, the odor of smoke still drifting down the corridor.

In the moments that followed, the once empty building suddenly swarmed with people. Para-medics and stretchers crowded the aisles. Men in various uniforms took up every inch of space. There were local policemen, the FBI and the US Marshals. She managed to find an empty office and collapsed on to a leather chair.

Voices. Noise. Confusion. Her cheek throbbed. Her heart hammered painfully against her ribs.

She wasn't certain if a minute or an hour passed before Corbin appeared in the doorway. Seeing him, knowing the worst was over, knowing they were both safe, unleashed a torrent of suppressed emotion.

As though sensing her distress, Corbin dragged her against his chest, and she cowered in the crook of his arm.

"You're all right," he soothed, stroking her hair. "You're all right."

She sniffled against his sleeve. She couldn't find her voice, couldn't seem to control her shaking.

He squeezed her shoulder, catching her hair beneath his hand.

"I have to answer some questions," he said. "I'll be right back, but I'm leaving someone to look out for you."

Not trusting her voice, she only nodded.

All too soon he was gone, and a paramedic was kneeling beside her. She was breathing rapidly, her body trembling. Though Beth was uninjured, the concerned young man wrapped a silver blanket around her shoulders and checked her pulse before administering oxygen.

The next twenty minutes passed in a blur.

Voices chattered around her, but she couldn't make out the words. She felt as though everyone was speaking in a foreign language.

A gurney rumbled past, the body covered, and her stomach lurched.

"Can you walk, ma'am?"

She glanced into the sympathetic gray eyes of a man wearing a coat that marked him as a US Marshal. "Yes."

"I'm Marshal Kirk. I'll be handling your case from here on out."

Her teeth chattered, and she clenched her jaw. "All right."

"He's a good man," a familiar voice spoke.

Corbin appeared, and tears burned behind her eyes. She grasped the key ring in her pocket. "I copied everything you need on this drive."

The marshal accepted the evidence with a wide smile. "You saved the day, Ms. Greenwood. Good work. Someone set a fire in the IT room. Crushed the servers with a baseball bat."

Corbin shrugged. "Looked like Van wasn't taking any chances. He was destroying the evidence as fast as you could download it."

"Then you got my note?" Beth asked.

"That was quick thinking on your feet, Ms. Greenwood," Corbin said. "Good work."

Marshal Kirk glanced between them. "Anything else you need, Ross?"

His expression sobered. "No." He hesitated, as though he might say something different, before taking a deep breath. "Like I said, I've worked with Marshal Kirk here before. He's good. The best. He'll take good care of you until we need your services. You and I will be working together to make sure we have all our ducks in a row. Shouldn't be more than a couple months, and you'll be back to your old life."

She understood. They'd be working together. But everything had changed. Everything was different. Otherwise, everything they'd accomplished was compromised.

The marshal nodded. "I've done this dozens of times before. You have nothing to worry about, ma'am. You won't be in witness protection for long. A couple of months, maybe. Just long enough to make sure we have everyone in custody."

Corbin glanced away.

"Great," she replied weakly.

The marshal shifted from foot to foot, and she took stock of the chaotic surroundings. Law enforcement was securing the scene. Everyone had a job. Everyone but her. Marshal Kirk was ready to be on his way. The time had come.

She didn't want this moment to end, because the next time they met, they'd be little more than strangers working together, and that was going to test all her fortitude.

She rose shakily to her feet. "I'm ready."

The marshal hesitated. "Why don't I meet you downstairs?"

Corbin nodded without looking at the man. "Sure."

Following the marshal's exit, they stood in awkward silence.

Corbin spoke first. "I'm sorry I wasn't there for you. Karli wouldn't stop talking, and then I spotted Van. I followed him when I should have been watching out for you."

"That wasn't your fault. I walked right in to Matt's office. Since I thought he hired me, I never even suspected him."

"Doesn't look like Van's bullet hit anything vital. He's going to live. You saved his life." Corbin gently touched her lip. "Van wasn't as fortunate."

She covered his fingers with her hand. "Thank you. For everything."

"You're gonna be all right, Beth."

She wanted something more. She wanted to press her cheek against his chest and let him hold her. She wanted to tell him how much he'd meant to her. But there were too many people. Too many eyes. She wouldn't risk his job.

Retracting her hand, she said, "So are you, Agent Ross."

Sorrow flickered in his eyes before he stuffed his hands in his pockets.

She turned. Keeping her head held high, she strode down the corridor. Saying goodbye to

Beth Greenwood wasn't going to be as easy this time around.

Because this time around she had someone she was going to miss.

THIRTEEN

Three months later, Homeland Security Head-quarters

Corbin stared at the letter in his hand, took a deep breath, and knocked on Baker's open door.

His superior waved him to one of the two seats set before his desk. "What's up?"

Corbin slid the paper across the shiny surface. "My resignation."

Baker pinched the corner between two fingers as though protecting evidence. "You sure this is what you want?"

"I'm positive."

"This about Beth Greenwood?"

Corbin ducked his head. "Yeah."

"She's out of witness protection as of last week. Case closed."

"I know."

Marshal Kirk had been correct in his assessment. The FBI had used the information to infiltrate the terrorist group, and the case against Quetech was settled quietly out of court. Everything was classified. The FBI was looking to catch bigger fish. Sam's killers had been brought to justice. One of the mercenaries was jailed, the other dead.

While Beth's analysis of the material had been invaluable, in order to protect the undercover operation, her testimony hadn't been needed.

"Your choice." Baker dropped the letter into his file drawer. "Just so happens I already have your replacement."

Corbin's eyes widened. "You knew?"

"Had a feeling. You've been moping around for months." Baker picked up his phone and barked, "Send in the new recruit," before setting down the receiver. "Found a real gem. Genius at numbers. Good instincts, too."

Corbin had expected an argument, or at least a little remorse. "I, uh, sure."

"Good."

This was better. No guilt. No baggage. The past three months had been transformative. He'd joined the men's group at his church and started volunteering again. After that, everything just seemed to fall into place. He'd spent two weeks visiting his parents. He'd spent time with his nephew. He'd taken the kid to the zoo. He hadn't been to the zoo in years. He'd made plans to visit in the future. Solid plans. Not vague promises.

He'd recognized that he wasn't nomadic by nature. He was, at heart, a family man. He'd find another job. He had some money saved. Maybe things wouldn't work out with Beth. Maybe they would. But he'd been patient for three long months, and he was ready to try.

If she didn't have feelings for him, he'd be devastated, but he'd move on. He'd survived before. He'd survive again. He wouldn't forgive himself unless he at least tried.

Baker glanced up. "Ah, here she is now."

Corbin recognized the floral scent of Beth's perfume before he turned around, and his heart slammed against his ribs.

Baker grinned at him. "Never thought I'd see the day when you were speechless."

Panic tripped along his nerve endings. This wasn't how he'd planned things. Well, actually, he hadn't planned anything. But he'd had plans to plan something.

She dropped on to the seat beside him, and his breath caught in his throat. He couldn't think.

"Here's the thing," Baker said, lumbering to his feet. "You can't fraternize with a witness, but there are no rules against office romance. Just keep the PDAs at home. I have a weak stomach." He reached into his desk drawer for Corbin's letter of resignation. "I have to recycle some papers. Can I add this?"

"Uh. Yeah. Sure."

"If you're staying, I'll have Fitzsimmons train her. I don't want her in your chain of command. Make HR happy."

Baker closed the door behind him.

A hand touched his sleeve. "What's wrong? You haven't even looked at me."

Hands shaking, he turned. "How? Why? I don't understand."

His breath caught. There was something different about her today. She was more beautiful than he remembered. She was vibrant. Her brilliant green eyes sparkled. Her lustrous hair was caught in the professional knot at the nape of her neck, and her crisp, dark suit rode up slightly on her bent knees. His gaze skittered away, and his mouth went dry.

She smiled. "After all the work we've done together over the past three months, Baker recruited me. I have a knack for this sort of thing."

Her eyes were soft and shimmering with something he couldn't quite identify. Affection?

He dropped to his knees before her chair and took her hands. "I was quitting. I—"

She cupped his cheeks, her expression tender. "Would you consider changing your mind? I think we'd work well together."

"A thousand times yes." He pressed his lips against her knuckles. "I'm crazy about you, Beth Greenwood. You're smart, funny and tough as nails. I adore the way you tap your heel against the floor when you're nervous. I want to eat mini donuts together whenever possible. I want to spend today, tomorrow and the tomorrow after that with you. I want to spend all my tomorrows with you."

"I hoped you'd say something like that." The hand against his cheek trembled. "I wasn't certain. But I had to try. I didn't know what you were feeling."

"I couldn't jeopardize the case. I hoped you'd understand."

"I did. I do. These past few months have been miserable. But we did it. We got 'em."

"*You* got 'em. None of this would have happened without you."

"I said that I didn't want to take second place to your job." She ducked her head. "But that was just an excuse. I sensed you were pulling away from me, and I was trying to protect myself. But I don't want to play it safe anymore. I want you. I know your work requires a lot of travel. A lot of time away. That's okay. I have my own work. You're worth waiting for."

He urged her to face him. "I don't want to run anymore. I've been running since Evan died. I thought I could outrun the grief, but I was wrong. It's like running from the dawn. The pain is there.

It'll always be there. But I finally realized that time doesn't actually heal, it's what we do with that time that brings healing. I have to believe that we all have the ability to make something good out of something awful. I have to believe God has a plan. I wish I could have known your dad, but I know he's a part of you. I'll know him through you."

Her eyes brimmed. "And I'll know Evan through you."

A sense of peace overtook him. "It took a while, but I finally understand. Everything changes, and that's okay. We're not the same people we were before we lost them, and I'm not the same person I was before I knew you. I'm different. I'm stronger. I'm better knowing you."

Blinking rapidly, she pressed a kiss against the bridge of his glasses. "I'm falling in love with you, Corbin, and I always finish what I start."

"Then let's start something beautiful. Together. I love you, Beth Greenwood, and I want to spend the rest of my life with you."

Lost in the wonder of his love, he kissed her, pouring his soul into the act, his hands running over the satiny smoothness of her hair. He'd been waiting his whole life for this, and he wasn't letting go.

He felt something against his cheek, and realized she was crying.

His stomach sank. "What's the matter? What's wrong?"

"Nothing. I'm happy. Blissfully, wonderfully

happy. But I just realized we've never even been on a date. An actual date. Maybe we should go for karaoke. Or coffee."

His heart resumed beating once more. "Definitely karaoke. We'll fly to Chicago and watch Janice sing 'Total Eclipse of the Sun.'"

"Deal. Then maybe we can get some coffee at that new shop on Fifth Street."

He stood and took her hand, leading her toward the door. "Deal."

She glanced around. "Where are we going?"

"To the airport. If I'm going to spend the rest of my life with you, I want to start dating right now. This moment."

She laughed. "You're crazy. This is my first day."

"I'll put in a good word with your boss."

"Okay, *Clark*." She faced him, and her expression softened. "Shouldn't you be able to fly us there yourself, superhero?"

He touched his glasses, his cheeks heating. "I'll get some new frames."

"Never." She placed her hand over his. "I love you just the way you are, Corbin Ross."

* * * * *

Dear Reader,

Welcome to my debut book in a different genre! Writing for Love Inspired Suspense has been a new and exciting adventure for me. For the past five years, I've been immersed in the historical old West. Switching from bonnets and wagons to cell phones and cyber security has been both challenging and fun.

No matter the genre, all writers have their own unique and personal method for creating plots and characters. For me, it's important that I see the opening scene clearly in my head. In *No Safe Place*, Beth Greenwood is facing a moral dilemma. The decision she makes at the beginning of the book transforms her life. I'm fascinated by stories involving ordinary people forced into extraordinary circumstances. I hope this book will be the first of many suspense adventures!

I love hearing from readers and would enjoy hearing your thoughts on this story. If you're interested in learning more about this book or other series I have written, I have more information on my website: sherrishackelford.com. I can also be reached by email at sherri@sherrishackelford. com, or at P.O. Box 116, Elkhorn, NE 68022.

Happy Reading!
Sherri Shackelford

Get 4 FREE REWARDS!

We'll send you 2 FREE Books plus 2 FREE Mystery Gifts.

Love Inspired® books feature contemporary inspirational romances with Christian characters facing the challenges of life and love.

FREE Value Over $20

Get 4 FREE REWARDS!

We'll send you 2 FREE Books plus 2 FREE Mystery Gifts.

Harlequin® Heartwarming™ Larger-Print books feature traditional values of home, family, community and—most of all—love.

FREE Value Over $20

READERSERVICE.COM

Manage your account online!

- Review your order history
- Manage your payments
- Update your address

> *We've designed the
> Reader Service website
> just for you.*

Enjoy all the features!

- Discover new series available to you, and read excerpts from any series.
- Respond to mailings and special monthly offers.
- Browse the Bonus Bucks catalog and online-only exculsives.
- Share your feedback.

Visit us at:

ReaderService.com